Collision of Worlds
Graveyard of Empires, Book II

by
Lincoln Cole

Published by Lincoln Cole, Columbus, 2016
LincolnJCole@gmail.com
www.LincolnCole.net

Cover Design by M.N. Arzu
www.mnarzuauthor.com

This one is for my friends, who sometimes tolerate me. Jeff, Jeff, Steve, and Dave.

"We live in a society exquisitely dependent on science and technology, in which hardly anyone knows anything about science and technology."

Carl Sagan

Prologue

Sector 4 – Tellus
Alaina Naylor

1

"When I went to the market today they didn't even have bread."

"No bread?" Carl Naylor echoed, raising an eyebrow toward his wife. "How could they run out of bread?"

They were both in the kitchen of their little home on Tellus in the capital city of Breitenberg preparing dinner. Carl stood at the sink trimming half-rotten vegetables, examining each carefully for glaring imperfections before dropping them into a bowl along with the others.

As Darius's rebellion went on these last two years, the tolerable level for rot and decay on these vegetables had loosened. Now, he was at the point that anything was 'acceptable' if he didn't feel it would make his family sick.

"I don't know. But they had none, and no one knew when they would be able to bake more."

"Damn," he said, dropping another spear of asparagus into the bowl. "Things just keep getting worse. First they ran out of most dairy products, and now bread."

"That isn't even the half of it," Kate replied. "By all accounts, the rationing has only just begun."

"What are they planning to cut back on next?"

"Meat, maybe," Kate answered. "Water? If it's something we need, they'll ration it or hike up the prices until we can't afford it."

"I'll get a second job if I have to," Carl said. "If we need the money."

"The money won't matter," Kate said, leaning heavily against the counter. "There won't be anything left to buy."

Alaina knelt in the living room next to the kitchen door, listening to her parents speak. She was supposed to be watching television but was really eavesdropping on her parents' conversation. She knew her parents didn't like her doing that, but she couldn't help herself.

They always assumed she didn't know what was going on out in the world and that she didn't understand grown-up things, but she did. She hated being treated like a seven-year-old girl.

Never mind that she was one.

In a short while, they would call her in for dinner to eat the meal they had prepared, but judging by the meager supplies her mother had returned home with from the market, Alaina knew it would be a small meal.

They were all small meals nowadays.

"The food lines are the worst of it," Kate continued. "Having to wait for hours and then only being allowed to purchase a small amount of anything. They only let you buy enough to take care of half of your family."

"I waited three hours for a cod filet yesterday," Carl agreed. "Three hours for one filet, and by the time I got there, they were all sold out. The woman three spots ahead of me got the last one. I've never felt so helpless in my entire life."

"How are we supposed to feed our children?" Kate asked. She was speaking lower now, and there was a thickness in her voice. Alaina had to strain to hear. "Or keep them clothed. I've had to mend Jessie's shirt three times in the last week."

A long moment passed, the only sound them working side by side. Alaina didn't like when her parents got sentimental like this, but it was a lot better than them being mad at each other. That happened a lot nowadays, too.

"We'll get by," Carl said finally. "It can't stay like this forever. The economy will make a turnaround."

"How?" Kate asked, a twinge of anger in her voice.

This was more what Alaina was used to.

"How can things possibly turn around? It's been two years since Tellus ratified the Union. Two years since our planet joined Darius and this stupid rebellion. The aid funding we used to receive from the Core is gone. Trade dried up. How are things going to get better?"

"Problems like this take time to correct," Carl argued.

"How much time? Do you know? Does Darius know? This war is costing us far more than it is costing the Republic."

"I know. Progress has been slow, but you saw the news. Big things are happening. More planets have sworn for the Union. Trade is starting back up in Sector Six. Darius is calculating, waiting for things to fall into place before launching an all-out military campaign against Axis and the First Citizen."

"How long can we wait? We are starving and can't take care of our families. By the time Darius decides we're ready to start fighting, we'll all be too weak to do anything. We should just end this: surrender and let us go back to the way things were."

"There is no turning back," Carl said quietly. "The only way for us now is forward."

"How are we supposed to keep up this rebellion? If Darius can't even keep his own people fed, how is he going to bring down the Republic?"

This time, her father was slower in responding.

"I don't know," he said. "Kate, I just don't know."

Kate sighed, breathing out the tension. "Neither do I. I know it isn't your fault...I just..."

"I understand," Carl said. "I supported Darius when he came to Tellus, but I'm not so sure anything will change now. But I promise I won't let you or the kids go hungry."

"How will you do that?"

The silence hung in the air. "The families of soldiers never go hungry."

"No, Carl," Kate said. "I won't let you. You promised you would never join or risk your life, and I *will not* let you."

"I know, but—"

"No," Alaina's mother interrupted sharply. "End of discussion."

Alaina heard her father blow out a breath of air, but he didn't say anything. She strained to hear, but it sounded like they were finished talking.

A few moments passed and then footsteps alerted her that they were heading toward the living room...where she was supposed to be watching cartoons.

She scurried back over to her spot on the floor. On the television two children were wandering through a make-believe forest, searching for stupid teddy bears or something. She pretended like it was funny as her parents pushed through the door and came inside.

"How's my big girl?" Carl asked, lifting Alaina up and giving her a hug.

He was disheveled and smelled of stale sweat. He spent long hours at work each day, coming home in the middle of the night, sometimes after she was asleep. She rarely saw him anymore, with how often he was working or waiting in the food lines.

She missed him.

"Hey, Daddy," Alaina said, squeezing him.

"What are you watching?"

"Cartoons," she answered.

He set her back on the floor and sat down on the couch. Her mother sat next to him, and it looked to Alaina like she'd been crying.

"How are your dance lessons going?" her father asked.

Alaina looked at the floor.

"We had to take her out of dance," her mother explained. "They closed shop because there were too few students. Everyone was behind on their payments."

"Oh, I'm sorry. I had no idea."

"It's okay, Daddy. I didn't like dance anyway."

"You didn't? I thought you loved it?"

"Nope," she said, kind of annoyed. She hadn't enjoyed her dance lessons for almost a month. "I want to learn how to fight."

Carl glanced at her mother, raising an eyebrow quizzically.

"Don't look at me. I don't know where she gets these ideas. Probably from vids."

Carl shrugged. "Maybe," he agreed. He turned back to Alaina. "So you want to learn how to fight, huh? Why? So you can be a superhero?"

She nodded emphatically. "I want to fight monsters."

"Don't worry, honey," her father said. "There aren't any real monsters."

"Oh, yes there are," Alaina said. "And I'm going to beat them up!"

He laughed. "Well, then I guess we had better eat dinner. We need to make sure you grow up big and strong to defeat the monsters."

Alaina was a little upset that he wasn't taking her seriously, but it didn't surprise her. Adults never really took the things she said seriously, but she knew that one day she would prove them all wrong and do everything she promised she would do.

There was suddenly a loud crashing sound in the distance, followed by a heavy rumbling noise that shook the whole house. The ground bounced under her feet, plates fell to the floor in the kitchen and shattered, and the windows began rattling.

Alaina screamed, covering her ears. Her father knelt on the floor next to her, wrapping her up in a tight hug and using his body to shield her. It lasted a full fifteen seconds, reverberating through the entire house before calming back down.

Once it was over, silence enveloped the living room, punctuated by the barking of dogs and screaming of sirens in the distance. She could feel her father holding her and panting in fear. Gradually, she pulled herself loose.

"What was that?" Kate asked breathlessly. She was clutching the couch, rising slowly on wobbling knees.

"I have no clue," Carl said. His face was ashen and Alaina had never seen him so afraid. "Maybe an explosion."

"An explosion? You don't think the Republic...?"

"No. No way," he replied. "We aren't under attack."

"How can you be—?"

"We would have heard something before today. They would have said something on the news if the Republic was on its way."

As he spoke, he moved over to the couch and flicked the remote to change the television station. Reports were rapidly being shown as all of the news outlets posted breaking news about what had just happened.

He selected a station, and the broadcast was set on an aerial view of the wreckage of an old building. It looked like an old warehouse, but there were no external markers denoting what it was for.

Fire licked the interior and half the building seemed to have been destroyed in an explosion. It was surrounded by containment crews and barricades. Firefighters were struggling to get it under control and put the flames out.

"A gas line malfunction," Carl read incredulously as the news captions scrolled past.

"Gas line?" Kate said. "Are you kidding?"

"That's the official story."

"There is no way a gas line did *that*," Kate said, gesturing angrily at the images on display. The camera began to pan left, and they saw a pile of long shapes under blankets. Alaina squinted, wondering what might be under the sheets.

Her father quickly turned the news back off.

"I know," he said. "Do they think we are stupid? That used to be an old chemical processing plant."

"They are probably testing a new weapon."

"Maybe," Carl said. "Or they might have been cutting costs in the chemical stores and had a malfunction. They've been sacrificing safety in there for years. This could just be a terrible accident."

Kate let out a huge sigh. "We keep seeing 'accidents' like this and we're just supposed to look the other way? We can't keep living like this."

"I know," Carl agreed.

"Constantly afraid," Kate continued. "Hungry. Despondent. We can't raise our family like this. We need to leave."

"Where?" Carl asked. His voice was low, full of defeat. "Where *will* we go, Kate? Where could we go that is better?"

"I don't know," she replied. "Off world?"

"Who would take us in? We are outcasts now, part of Darius's rebellion. Every other planet in Sector Six is as bad off as we are, and no one else would let us come. At best we are fools. At worst, traitors."

"Maybe this was all just wrong," she said. "Joining Darius and his rebellion; joining the Union: maybe it was all just a terrible mistake that we're paying for."

"It was," Carl agreed softly. "Supporting Darius was the worst decision we've ever made as a planet. I wanted freedom for our children, but I didn't really understand how bad things would get. Now we're all going to pay."

Alaina could barely believe her ears. Normally, when her parents argued about Darius and the rebellion, her father wasn't willing to give an inch. He thought joining the Union was the right and only choice. It was the idealist choice, the one best for the future.

How bad must things be, then, for him to take her mother's side?

"Maybe it was all a mistake," her father reiterated. "And we will lose everything. I honestly don't know. What I *do* know is that there is nothing we can do now except move forward. We can only do the best we can with what we're given."

"I know," Kate said. She pulled Carl close and pressed her face into his chest. "But at what cost?"

Chapter 1
Sector 6 - Alderson
Jayson Coley

1

"Is it heavy?"

"Not particularly," Jayson said, moving his arms to test the way the armor moved. It glided with his motions, feeling more like he was wearing a long-sleeved shirt than a few hundred pounds of body armor.

"It looks heavy."

Jayson shrugged. "It's actually quite comfortable."

"You'll need to put the helmet on before the environment seals are in place and climate controls click on," Alexander Robertson explained, standing off to the side and watching.

He was an old man with a flowing white beard and wrinkles. He walked with a cane, but Jayson knew from experience that it was mostly for show and defense; he certainly knew how to use it, and he wasn't the sort of man to be trifled with.

"Climate controls?" Jayson asked.

Alexander nodded. "The suit will protect you against most elements and is actually quite comfortable. It is nothing compared to the tech we used to put on the Fists, but bringing it down to your size meant we had to drop some of the bulkier items."

He glanced over at the other person standing with them: Maven Ophidian, the woman who was in charge of the Academy. They had rarely seen her these past two years, and each time he did, he felt uneasy.

She wore a black robe that covered her entire body and dragged around an oxygen tank. A mask covered her face and made sucking noises as it pumped air into her lungs.

The only part of her he could see were her eyes, and they were cold and empty. She watched them and studied them but rarely spoke.

They were standing in a field outside of the Academy on one of the nicest days of the season. Winter was just around the corner, and they'd learned from experience just how devastatingly cold it could get.

"When do I get a suit?" Richard asked. He was a big and burly man with an infectious laugh. He shaved more often now, something Tricia demanded of him, but Jayson didn't like seeing him without his beard. It made him look like his head was too small for his body.

"This is a prototype," Alexander said. "We're testing how well the components work in relation to each other. It won't be ready for production for at least ten more years."

"So...not anytime soon?" Richard asked.

"No," Alexander said.

"Drat."

"What else does it do?" Jayson asked, moving the rest of his body. He could hardly believe how smooth it felt, like the hydraulics were supporting him rather than the other way around.

"It keeps you alive. We are testing out a few targeting systems."

"And the cloaking," Maven chimed in, her voice raspy and deep.

An uncomfortable look flashed across Alexander's face. "We...were forced to abandon the cloaking. It is included in this prototype, but the energy expenditure will be too much for the suit to handle. It only lasts for a few seconds before it needs to be recharged."

She stared at him for a long moment, the only sound the tank helping her breathe. "Show me."

Alexander nodded and turned to Jayson. "Put the helmet on. It won't work unless you are sealed."

Jayson did as he was told, sliding the helmet on over his head. As soon as it locked into place, he heard a whooshing sound as air was expelled.

A voice spoke up from inside the helmet. The voice was dry and boring, that of an old and tired-sounding man. "All systems are functional. Awaiting commands."

"What was that?" he asked.

"That is your onboard intelligence system," Alexander explained. "On your right palm, you'll find an indentation. Flick your thumb across it."

Jayson felt around, quickly finding the indentation. He pressed his thumb into it. Nothing happened.

"It is a practiced motion," Alexander said. "You must do it quickly."

Jayson swiped a few times, but still there was no response. Finally, he was able to flick it, and he heard a humming sound.

Otherwise, though, nothing seemed to happen. The humming lasted for a few seconds and then dissipated. "Did it work?" he asked.

When he glanced over at Richard, he saw a look of shock on his friend's face. "It worked. You disappeared."

"What do you mean?"

"I mean, there was an outline of you, sort of, but I could see right through you."

"It uses light absorption and image distortion. There are limitations to *how* we see things, and this suit takes advantage of it. Works only minimally against technology but well against people."

"That is freaking awesome," Richard said. "I want one."

"It drains the suit's power rather quickly. We have a shutoff in place, and the cells recharge, but we can't put a bigger capacitor in place or we run the risk of an errant shot causing the suit to explode."

Maven studied Jayson for a moment and then nodded. "Very well. Continue looking into the technology, and we will revisit the issue. For now, you can leave it out of future prototypes. What about the armor itself? Is it sturdy?"

"We have tested it in contained environments and it is rated up to—"

Maven casually walked over to a nearby table and picked a pistol up. She eyed it for a second, turned, and fired at Jayson.

The shot was loud and he felt the bullet hit him squarely in the chest, staggering him back. It didn't do any real damage, though, and the bullet absorbed most of the impact.

The disheartening part was what if it hadn't?

"You shot me?" he asked, glancing down at the torn armor. He saw the armor shifting and molding where the bullet had impacted. "What the hell is that?"

"The armor is self-repairing," Alexander explained, eyeing Maven warily. "It will continue trying to repair any damage to a certain point, though occasionally raw materials will be necessary to replace lost matter. As I was saying, the armor is bulletproof up to a certain rating, but we haven't tested anything—"

Maven ignored him. She turned back to the table and picked up a rifle. Jayson felt his eyes go wide and started backing up, trying to get away. She turned, aimed, and pulled the trigger before he could take more than a few steps.

This time, the armor didn't absorb all of the impact. He felt himself get thrown back a few meters. He landed hard on his back and felt a sharp impact on his chest, taking his breath away.

He lay there, looking up at the sky and trying to breathe for a few seconds. Richard appeared above him, shouting something with a concerned expression on his face, but all Jayson could see were little dots floating around his head.

After a few minutes, he felt his breathing pick back up, and the world started coming back into focus. Richard helped him sit up.

"You all right?"

He shook his head. "No," he said, his voice wispy. His chest was in agony, and he felt like he was bleeding.

Richard reached down and plucked the shell out of his chest. "Didn't really make it through," he said, eyeing the wound. "Another centimeter, though..."

The shell was the size of Jayson's fist and looked like it had been flattened.

They all turned and looked at Maven, who was still holding the rifle in her hands. She gently set the gun back on the table.

"It works," she said, nodding at Alexander. "Let me know when we can make more."

Then, she turned and strode off, heading back into the Academy.

2

"She's crazy," Richard said, shaking his head once she was gone.

"Maybe," Alexander agreed, a weary expression on his face. "But, in my experience, most people with her power usually are. And, if they aren't, then they become crazy somewhere along the way."

"That hurt like hell," Jayson said, trying to stand up. The other two men helped him, lifting him to his feet. "When you asked if I wanted to test out some new armor..."

"When she brought guns, I assumed they were for *you* to shoot to see the armor in action. I would have preferred that test to be on the empty suit."

They spent the next few minutes stripping the armor back off of Jayson and checking over his chest. He had a huge welt at the bottom of his ribs, and he wouldn't have been surprised if a couple of them had been cracked.

But, all in all, it wasn't too terrible and he was fairly certain he would be just fine in a couple of weeks.

"Do I get to keep the armor?" he asked.

Alexander smiled sadly at him and shook his head. "No. Not yet at least. We will need to test it in the field soon, but there are still some kinks we need to work out with this suit before it is field ready."

"Damn," Jayson said. "Any word yet on when we're being sent out?"

"Nothing," Alexander replied. "But don't worry, I'm sure Maven has something large in store for you."

He nodded at them both and then headed back to the Academy.

Jayson glanced over at Richard and saw an equally worried expression on his face.

"Maven having something planned for us is what worries me."

Chapter 2
Sector 6 - Jaril
Oliver Atchison

1

The speakers of the little box-shaped freighter, *Cudgel*, chimed. It made a high-pitched whistling sound, alerting the two men sitting inside the haphazardly-converted shipping bay that they had received a new message.

"Another one?" Jim Crater muttered, not looking up from the stack of papers resting in front of him.

He was a grizzled man in his late forties with leathery skin and gray hair. He moved slowly and with a pronounced limp from a wound sustained a few years earlier in a shootout. It was a shootout, in fact, that he'd helped to incite. He was also, Oliver had learned, a very intense man in everything he did.

Which was a polite way of saying he got angry at the drop of a hat.

That wasn't all bad, though. He wasn't physical with his anger, more prone to sulking and complaining than lashing out, and it gave him a presence that made people stop and take notice.

Right now, however, he just looked tired and old. He hadn't slept much in the last few weeks since everything in his life had started to fall apart. He just moved around the *Cudgel* like a phantom, refusing to go out in public for fear of being recognized or mocked.

Oliver, on the other hand, loved to go out and get recognized. That was why he spent so much money on clothing and accessories;

he wanted to stand out. It wasn't *necessarily* why he spent so much time grooming or visiting day spas, but it was a contributing factor to be sure.

Jim had been poring over these incoming messages for the last several hours, and Oliver could tell that his friend was exhausted and running on fumes. He was overwhelmed by the sheer scale of what he was trying to accomplish, especially when there was nothing he could actually do in his current position. It was eating away at him.

"Looks like," Oliver agreed. "More people who want to join the crew of Admiral Jim Crater."

Jim winced at the title, Oliver noticed. It had been a badge of honor for him during the first months of his Admiralty, but now it had become something of a mockery. Reality had finally settled in for him, and he was coming to terms with the truth of his situation.

Oliver flicked open his lighter and held the flame to his pipe. He puffed a few times, watching the glow inside the bowl until the tobacco was lit just right. His was an exquisite and expensive pipe, gaudy and pristine, and certainly one of his most expensive possessions.

He considered the purchase to be well worth it, though. Buying expensive things—especially when the right people *knew* they were expensive—was a mark of station in many circles.

Those were the circles he wanted to be a member of. Like his clothes—fiber cloth that shimmered as he walked—the ostentatious pipe was a testament to his newfound status in life.

2

He hadn't grown up around wealth or privilege, but he *had* studied it for many years. He understood that ninety percent of what separated the privileged from the masses was affectation—with enough money and ambition, he could fake anything.

"How am I supposed to go through all of these?" Jim asked, rubbing his face with his hands. "There are hundreds of applications here."

"You aren't supposed to," Oliver replied. "That's the point. If you don't have the means to hire any of these people, then don't torture yourself by acknowledging them."

"These are the very people I *should* acknowledge," Jim argued. "They are seeking me out because I mean something to them. They are personally offering their services, and many of them chose me directly out of school and basic training rather than Hektor Menshen and his fleet."

"They chose you because they think there is a future with your fleet," Oliver replied. "If you just admitted you weren't recruiting, people would stop applying."

"I can't do that. If I admit that I don't *have* a fleet, then Hektor has already won."

Oliver shrugged. "Sometimes that's what it comes down to. You can't keep playing the game when the other team won't share the ball."

"I didn't even post a bulletin to say we were opening up recruitment. Why would so many people send in their applications now?"

"If I had to guess, I would say Hektor had something to do with it. He wants to embarrass you."

"You think he would stoop so low?"

"I don't think it's stooping for him. This is just who he is."

It had been just under two years since Jim and Oliver had stumbled into the wealth and power of their new positions. They had been the first citizen responders to the 'attack' from the Republic. They helped chase Vivian and the Republic fleet away from the planet.

Their faces had been emblazoned on every news outlet and vid screen for weeks, and they were instantly turned into heroes.

Oliver would be forever grateful to Jim for bringing him along that day.

Even after Jim shot him in the chest.

3

It didn't hurt anymore, but it was rather embarrassing. Sure, he took the shot on behalf of the Royal Family and to save all of Jaril (so they thought), but it was still difficult dealing with the jokes at his expense. Jim was the folk hero, and Oliver was just the sidekick who could take a shot to the chest and live to tell about it.

The Royal Family had spared no expense in thanking and congratulating the two men, parading them around the entire planet and showering them in accolades. They lived on cloud nine for several months after the events.

But, whereas Oliver understood that what they achieved was temporary fame, Jim was of the opinion that they would be able to springboard their newfound status and recognition into something greater.

And, for a while, he had been right. He had reached for the clouds, scooped up a handful, and was watching it disintegrate between his fingers.

The speakers chimed as another message was logged onto the system. It sounded—almost—like it was taunting them.

"Quite the busy day," Oliver offered, breaking the silence. "That's the fourth application in so many minutes. Are you sure you want to read them all?"

Jim only groaned in response.

"Why not take a break? Get some fresh air and forget about this for a while. The applications won't be going anywhere anytime soon."

"They help distract me."

"From what?"

"From remembering how great things were months ago."

Oliver didn't have a good answer for that. He still remembered those first few weeks. Dozens of spectators saw him get blasted in the market. He'd been in the hospital, and everyone thought the attack had come from the Republican operative. He was even awarded a medal for being wounded in the line of duty.

Then everything went terribly wrong. Jim decided to press too hard and asked for a ranking position in the military. He'd served for years before leaving on less-than-honorable terms, and he wanted all of that respect back. He leveraged his public support by demanding that the Royal Family reinstate him at a higher rank than he left despite his injuries.

The public had backed him. Millions came out to support him in his bid as he gained the backing of a separatist movement that felt they should elect officials, not honor the Royal Family. Jim got enough support that getting reinstated became an inevitability.

Which would have been where it ended, but meanwhile the Royal Family had quietly investigated the circumstances around the attack in the market. It didn't take them long to discover exactly what had happened, and that Jim had been the one to orchestrate everything.

That's when the men in black suits paid them a visit.

4

Not a gentle visit, either. Both of them had spent nearly a month locked in a secret prison while the Royal Family tried to decide what to do with them. Oliver had been fairly certain that they would be quietly eliminated.

Public opinion was on their side, and the Royals knew that exposing the pair as frauds would create backlash, as some people would believe it was a conspiracy. They couldn't make Jim Crater into an enemy without angering the lay people, so they did the next best thing.

They made him family.

It would have been a public relations fiasco if they admitted that the Republic had never initiated a conflict in the market. Instead, the Royal Family decided to take credit for what happened.

After a series of back room discussions and blackmail, the Royal Family officially adopted Jim Crater. They tied his fate to theirs and quieted all of the naysayers who felt that the Royal Family was ignoring the voice of the people.

More importantly, they filled a vacant position of great importance that they knew would excite Jim. They didn't just give him his position in the military back: they made him an Admiral.

The new position hypothetically made Jim one of the three most important military leaders in the entire Kingdom, but only figuratively. The problem was, the positions were not supported monetarily by the Royal Family but rather independently. The armies were loyal to the Indeil Kingdom but maintained and controlled by the Admirals themselves.

The title meant nothing without support and funding. Jim didn't have a fleet, and he didn't have enough money to build or buy a fleet. Worse, considering everything that had happened, he certainly couldn't ask anyone who did have money for help.

Worse still, it angered the other Admirals and put Jim in the awkward position of being powerless but with powerful enemies. Jim didn't have any family ties or political background to maintain this new position. It didn't take long for him to realize that although money could buy influence, it was only a small piece of the puzzle in the larger political arena.

Oliver knew that his friend had no idea the Royal Family was manipulating him. Jim had been thrilled about everything, but he floundered under the weight of his new position and gradually slipped into obscurity.

Now, unbeknownst to Jim, he was about to lose it all.

5

Oliver puffed on his pipe, watching the flame spread deeper into the dried leaves. He looked at his friend on the opposite side of the table through a cloud of hazy smoke.

He'd heard the rumors from a few of his high-powered friends that Jim Crater's days were numbered. The Royal Family was considering revoking his position as Admiral, which would basically be a death sentence for Jim.

He had reached for the stars but had only managed to burn his hand.

Oblivious, Jim simply kept looking over the resumes of soldiers he could never enlist.

"Are you almost finished?" Oliver asked.

Jim looked up, his eyes angry and bloodshot. "Not even close. I've got at least two dozen more to look at, and they just keep coming in."

"You should at least turn the sound off," Oliver said as it chimed again.

Each time the speakers made their little noise, Jim winced. It was psychological torture.

"You could help," Jim said, narrowing his eyes.

"I am," Oliver replied.

"You haven't looked at a single dossier since they started coming in."

Oliver shrugged. "Emotional support?"

Jim sighed, turning back to the data pad he was looking at.

"You know you can't hire any of them, right?" Oliver explained, trying to reach through and wake Jim up from his delusions. "You don't have the funds to pay them, nor a single job to actually keep any of them busy. This is a wasted effort."

"Once I buy a Verdana class ship, I'll be able to—"

"You won't get one," Oliver argued. "The *Cudgel* is probably the only ship you'll ever own, and I still own half of it."

"I have enough money to purchase a Verdana. Maybe even a Capital."

"Do you? Most of your funds were expended last year solidifying the Admiralty. How much money could you have left?"

"I have plenty, and if I need more, I can get a loan. No bank would refuse to loan money to an Admiral."

"No Admiral would stoop so low as to beg for money."

"Not from a bank," Jim said.

The words hung in the air. Oliver laughed, resting his pipe on the table.

"You mean from me?"

"You've been doing quite well, by all reports, with your trading business."

Smuggling, actually.

But Oliver wasn't about to correct him. He certainly was doing well, and had made a fortune these last two years, but that was because he was a shrewd businessman who didn't make bad investments.

Jim was a good friend but a bad investment.

"I don't have any cash on hand. It's all funneling back into the business. In five years' time, the assets will mature and I'll have a lot of capital, but right now I can barely rub two credits together."

"In five years, you're going to have a fortune? And what will I have? We're in this together, remember."

"You have an invested stake in all of my profits, and you are an Admiral, remember? I think you were quite well compensated."

"An Admiral without a fleet. The *Cudgel* is half mine, too," Jim said. "You've been using it to trade with Terminus, and I haven't seen any profits."

"Because it's all invested," Oliver reiterated. "I'll pay you your fair share once we are able to cash out, but not yet. I hired four new pilots and contracted two more trading vessels in the last month. Right now, I'm building demand by selling cheap, but it won't be long until we're raking in the credits."

"And then you'll try to cheat me out of my cut?"

The words stung, and Oliver felt a burst of anger.

"I'm your *only* friend and the *only* contact you have with the outside world. Are you sure you want to sever that tie, too?"

"You cheat everyone," Jim replied. "Why wouldn't you try to steal from me?"

"I've *never* cheated you, and I think you've fared pretty damn well since we met."

"So I'm supposed to trust you?"

"I'm willing to buy out your stake in the *Cudgel* the *very* second you decide to sell," Oliver replied angrily. "And when I do, you can pack your bags and get the hell off my ship. But, while we are business partners, I'm not going to cheat you, and I'm offended you would even suggest it."

Jim let out a sigh. "I know, Olly. I'm just…I'm just frustrated. I'm sorry, I didn't mean it."

Oliver leaned back in his chair and let out a breath of air. He knew that Jim meant every word of it, but it wasn't worth holding grudges over petty words.

The thing was, Jim was right: Oliver wouldn't *necessarily* cheat him, but he would find ways to make sure numbers worked out in his favor. Oliver wasn't going to cheat Jim out of his *entire* share…just, you know, part of it.

"No worries, Jim. It's fine."

"I just desperately wanted for all of *this* to work," Jim continued. "The Admiralty. I see all of these people who want to join our crew and the potential of what we *could* do, and then the sobering reality of where we are hits me, and I start to feel sick. I mean, you've been able to make some money and we've done well, but imagine what we could *really* do. We could change the entire damn Kingdom."

"But we *can't*," Oliver said. "No one is going to help us."

"Which is why I keep sending these recruits, a 'Thanks, but no thanks' response after viewing their application. But, just once, I'd like to be able to respond by saying, 'Yes, you can start tomorrow' instead of turning them all away."

"Maybe you just need to relax. Take a break and get some fresh air. It's beautiful today."

"I thought it was raining."

"It did overnight, but it stopped this morning. Now it's sunny but not too hot. You should go get a breath of fresh air. Take a walk."

"Maybe you're right," Jim agreed. "I can barely even think straight anymore."

"You've been cooped up for days."

"Yeah, I know." Jim looked up at Oliver. "Wait, this last message wasn't an application. It is one of those party invitations."

"Oh? Haven't seen one of those in ages."

Jim handed the data pad across the table to Oliver. He read it over quickly. "A banquet invitation from Sir Fergus Cortet."

"They want you to go?" Jim asked.

Oliver shook his head. "They want *you* to go. The letter is for the Captain of the *Cudgel*. Though, it does mention that the First Officer is also invited. First Officer, eh? I like that. Can I be your First Officer?"

"Sure, why the hell not?"

"The invitation looks legitimate. It bears the Cortet family seal," Oliver said.

"I thought Fergus Cortet was dead?"

"Not quite, but I think he's close. He has a daughter, so maybe this is actually a gathering for her."

"A daughter? How old is she?"

Oliver pulled out a data pad and ran a quick search. "Doesn't say anywhere online. They must be monitoring and curating information about the family."

"Must be a reclusive bunch."

"Yep. Your kind of people. They are powerful, though, if they're able to remove information from the web and keep themselves hidden from the public. The only news report I can find about her at all says she's twelve, but that was a few years ago and is doubtless intentional misinformation."

"So she's probably just a kid?" Jim asked.

"It's possible. Maybe this is her birthday party," Oliver offered.

"Then why invite me?"

"Maybe they don't know that you stopped getting invitations like this several months ago."

"Could be."

"Or maybe they *do* know about your situation, and she wants you to come and entertain them."

Jim chuckled and leaned back in his chair, rubbing his eyes. "So she wants me to come so they can mock me? Am I supposed to be her clown?"

Oliver laughed. "Maybe if you go wearing a red nose, she'll give you a ship."

"Not funny."

"It's a little funny."

"They must have grown tired of mocking me behind my back and want to put me down face to face."

"Or maybe they have a business proposal for you."

Jim thought about that. "Not likely," he said. "Why not just tell me in the letter instead of inviting me to a gathering?"

"You really have no idea how high culture works, do you?"

"In any case, I'm too busy to attend."

"Busy doing what? Looking through your overqualified applicants?"

Jim picked up the data pad and scrolled to the application he was currently looking at. "Dramatically overqualified. This guy is trained to operate planetary weaponry."

"The kind of weapons the *Cudgel* could fly inside the barrel of?"

"Yep."

"We should buy one of those."

Jim ignored him, scrolling to another application. "And *this* guy is a master ranked pilot up to Verdana class ships."

"A pilot would be nice," Oliver said. "I mean, I'm serviceable, but I'm always afraid I'm going to crash."

"How long do you think he would stick around when he found out what he was going to be flying? As soon as he signed on and saw this pile of junk, he would turn and run the other way."

Oliver couldn't disagree. So far, most people didn't know how bad things were for Jim as an Admiral and member of the Royal Family. They still thought he had the support of the king and queen and was in charge of a fleet of ships.

That was the fairytale version of events. Jim couldn't exactly tell everyone that his fleet consisted of a single ship. If someone came aboard and reported back how bad things really were...

Well, that would end Jim's aspirations very quickly.

Might be worth looking into, Oliver decided. Better to crush his dreams now than let him continue floundering in despair.

"But look at these," Jim added, grabbing up another data pad with its own list of applicants. "Martin here says he spent four years training to be a veterinarian before he realized his education was just God's way of teaching him to kill people. Sally is a ballerina who repeatedly compares herself to a praying mantis."

"Not exactly an encouraging image," Oliver agreed.

"And Steve," Jim continued, grabbing another and thrusting it across the table at Oliver. "Steve here wrote a goddamn poem! About me!"

Oliver glanced at it and burst out laughing. "He compares you to an Esson."

"What the hell is an Esson?"

"A type of flower," Oliver said, laughing again. "One that smells like blueberries."

"What is wrong with these people?" Jim asked, sighing again.

"They just really want to serve on your ships," Oliver explained. "You are an Admiral who came from nothing: proof that everyone's wish can come true if they just work hard enough."

"It isn't true, though," Jim argued. "I'm a farce."

"But you serve the purpose of cajoling the masses. People look up to you, and it's better than having them rebel against the Royal Family."

"Why would they look up to me?"

"Because you're not an arrogant asshole and off-putting like Hektor Menschen or Brutus Volt. Those Admirals have reputations for being elitist and looking down on people. People don't see you that way. You're a man of the people and for the people."

"Sure," Jim said, sighing. "At the very least, I'm way down here with the people."

Oliver stood up and grabbed his overcoat, tamping out his pipe and slipping it into his pocket.

"Where are you going?" Jim asked.

Oliver pointed to the data pad with the invitation to the Cortet gathering.

"I have a party to go to at the Cortet residence. You know, since I am your First Officer and all," Oliver said. "I'll just tell them I'm there representing your interests."

"Oh God, I take it back. You aren't my First Officer, and you sure as hell don't represent me."

"Too late," Oliver said. "No takebacks."

Jim sighed. "Fine. Do you really want to go, though, knowing what we know about these bloodsuckers?"

Oliver shrugged. "If they want a clown, then I'll go be the best damn clown I can be. Who knows, maybe I'll get something useful in return. You can't succeed if you don't try."

"You also can't fail."

Oliver paused in the doorway before looking back at his miserable friend. He missed the vitality of Jim in those early days when he first became an Admiral. He'd been hopeful and driven, ready to seize his place in the world and overcome all obstacles.

And now he was a shell of that man, a pitiful middle-aged failure waiting for people he had learned were his betters to take their gifts back. He'd been completely and utterly defeated.

"That's a sad way to live your life," Oliver said, disappearing from the cargo hold.

Of course, it wasn't that Oliver considered himself much better. He wasn't going to this party as a noble gesture or to push back against the oppressors trying to hold him down. Oliver didn't like lying to Jim about his motives for going to the Cortet residence, but he knew that if he mentioned the reason, Jim would be furious and inconsolable.

His own desires about what he might achieve, unlike his friend's, were enticed by this invitation, but for a completely different reason than monetary gain.

He just hoped she would be there.

Chapter 3
Sector 6 - Willamond
Vivian Drowel

1

Vivian set the digital book down on the copilot's chair when the comm rang through. Her feet were propped up on the terminal of her little ship, and she was beginning to feel sleepy.

She hated to read, and she had a special hatred for nonfiction books about how to raise children. She'd read dozens of them in these last two years, and all of the advice was starting to blend together.

But she was determined to absorb as much of it as she could. Everything she'd learned about children from the Ministry was wrong, she knew, which meant she had to be prepared for anything that happened with Traq until he was an adult.

Worse, she also had to worry about how to handle things that would *never* be in these silly books. He was different than normal children, and even different from the ones who were discovered and brought into the *Ordo Mens Rea*. She would need to be prepared for anything and everything that happened with him.

She realized, however, that she hadn't actually retained the last several pages of this most recent book. It was boring and dry, talking about the stages a child would go through before becoming an adult.

Maybe a break was a good thing.

With a yawn, she clicked the button to accept the call. Argus Wade's face appeared on screen. He was back at the Ministry, she knew, covering for her and dealing with his own problems.

He looked haggard, older than the last time she'd spoken with him. They rarely communicated anymore for fear of being overheard by the Ministry. Things would go very badly for Wade if they found out that he was helping her hide Traq from them.

"Wade?"

"Hi, Viv," Argus Wade said.

"You look like hell."

"Thanks," he said, rubbing his face with his hands. "I haven't really slept in the last few weeks. I keep expecting them to break down my door. Drag me away to a white room with ice picks."

"You have a vivid imagination," Vivian said.

"Not so vivid," Wade replied. Vivian could see from the expression on his face that something terrible had happened. "*Denigen's Fist* is on its way to the Core."

Vivian sat up, her feet landing on the floor with a thud. Suddenly she was wide awake.

"Abigail?"

Wade nodded. "I don't know what the Minister is planning...or if he's planning anything at all. But I can't think straight right now."

"It's been two years," Vivian said. "If the Minister was going to do something about this, he would have already."

"I think he knows."

"I doubt it. He isn't a patient man."

Argus didn't seem convinced, but he didn't disagree. "In any case, this is the first time *Denigen's Fist* has been back to Sector One. If the Minister has something planned, it's going to happen soon."

"You think he is going to...?"

She didn't finish the thought, but the unspoken sentiment hung in the air between them. Wade sighed.

"Officially, she was never enrolled in the *Ordo Mens Rea*, so as far as the books and records are concerned, she's just an ordinary girl serving as the Ministerial Envoy aboard a Capital Class Ship...which is strange enough on its own, considering her age, but nothing anyone could do anything about."

"So they don't know?"

"No, not officially. Unofficially, though, I'm fairly certain the Minister knows everything. He just has no evidence to act upon."

"But, she's his Envoy. He doesn't have any direct control over her while she is on *Denigen's Fist*."

34

"No, he technically can't do anything while she's on that ship, at least not without creating a scandal and admitting that she was appointed behind his back and without his consent. It would make him look bad. Publicly, his hands are tied."

"So you're safe?"

"Not exactly. He can't publicly do anything, but I'm certain he has something planned in retribution. He isn't going to forget, and he certainly won't forgive."

"He doesn't always do things publicly," Vivian added. "And he's got the full power of the Ministry behind him."

Argus held up his hands. "That's why I can't sleep."

"You did what you thought was necessary," Vivian said. "To protect your child."

"Did I?" Wade said, shaking his head. "Do you really think *this* was the best thing for Abigail? After Daer..."

His voice trailed off. Vivian knew what he was talking about because the events of Daer had become living legend everywhere throughout the galaxy. Overnight, it seemed that everyone knew the name of Captain Kristi Grove and her execution of two-thousand criminals.

Doubtless, that was why she had done it. She wanted to make a name for herself and build up a reputation. That mission was accomplished.

Rumors also spoke about the Envoy who sanctioned the killings on behalf of the Ministry. A mere child, but bloodthirsty and terrible. No one would dare speak negatively of her in public, but she knew their sentiments. Many viewed Abigail as a return to darker times hundreds of years ago when the Ministry had free rein to kill as it saw fit.

"You couldn't have known," Vivian said. "No one could have anticipated what Captain Grove had planned."

"She's turning my daughter into a puppet. And there's nothing I can do about it. She used me, Vivian."

"But the alternative was far worse," Vivian said. "The Minister might know what you did, but he can't prove it without compromising himself as well. Captain Grove might be using Abigail for some personal crusade, but it's better than Abigail being killed...or worse."

"I know," Wade said, "it's just that..."

Vivian nodded and didn't press the issue. She decided to change the subject. "What about Traq? Does the Minister know of him as well?"

"He doesn't. Of that I'm completely certain. It seems he forgot about you in the preceding years. He's probably been spending so much time trying to find new ways to punish me."

"I suppose there are more pressing issues than a rogue member of the *Ordo Mens Rea*. At least I haven't raised an army against the Republic."

Wade nodded. "Darius is growing in power. He has fifteen loyal planets in his Union now."

"All in Sector Four?"

"A few are actually in Sector Three. People are either completely loyal to Darius or terrified of him. He murdered Captain Queston."

"Murdered? Why?"

"Does Darius need a reason? He hijacked Queston's fleet and killed thousands of the crew. The First Citizen is starting to take him seriously, but it gets worse."

"What do you mean?"

"People are starting to ask questions about his time in the Ministry before he started the Union. People want to know what his past is, and they want to know about the *Ordo Mens Rea*."

Vivian was silent for a long moment, thinking over the ramifications of that. The *Ordo Mens Rea* was one of the best-kept secrets in the entire galaxy, and people had died for simply speaking too loudly about it.

But, if lay people knew Darius was a member of it before leaving and wanted to know more, it could unravel the entire sadistic network the Ministry had built. The Minister would kill every single member, including the children, to keep it from turning into a scandal.

"What's going to happen?" Vivian asked.

"I don't know. The Minister is paranoid. Not a single child from the recent batch of recruits was accepted into the Order," he said.

Vivian felt her stomach clench.

"None?"

"There were twenty-seven with the genetic marker who showed up. The youngest was three years old. Now there are twenty-seven more Keepers."

"He can't just do that," Vivian protested. "That's..."

"Insane?"

"I was going to say genocidal."

"He *can* do it, and he is," Wade replied with a sigh. "Twenty more members of the Order just fled last week to join Darius. The Minister is using that as his justification for his heavy-handed actions. It's creating a bad cycle. More leave because he cracks down, so he cracks down harder. It's bad, Vivian."

She nodded. She'd known things could turn ugly after Darius left—very few people in the *Ordo Mens Rea* felt any real loyalty to the Ministry—but she didn't think it would get so bad this quickly.

"So what do we do?"

"We keep our heads down. The Union can't challenge the Aristocracy, and from all reports, Darius is running out of support and funds. The First Citizen has sent his best Shields to assassinate Darius. One of them will catch up with him eventually. He'll die in a gutter, forgotten and alone, and people will forget about the Union. Then things will return to normal."

Vivian wasn't sure she believed him. The Aristocracy was old. Stale. A lot of people weren't content with the way things were being managed, and the cancers of their society ran deep. Trying to purge them might end up doing more harm than good.

And, if normal people found out the full extent of what the *Ordo Mens Rea* was...if they knew what dark and twisted truths the Ministry was withholding from them...

"Speaking of things that aren't normal," Wade said, "where is Traq?"

"Outside," Vivian said. She leaned forward in her chair, pushing her hair back from her face. "You know, I'm really starting to get the hang of this parenting thing, Wade."

"Oh yeah?"

"Yeah. I've read a dozen books so far on how to raise Traq properly. They all have different theories, but it boils down to basically the same idea: preparing him to survive in the world once he leaves the nest, so to speak."

"Uh huh," Wade said. "That's really all there is to it."

"So it's really just training, like the training we went through at the Ministry and then what I experienced to become a Shield. If I can pass along my knowledge to him, then he's going to be fine."

"Well, not exactly like we went through, right?" Wade asked with a shrug. "I mean, he isn't even seven years old yet. He doesn't need to go through anything like that."

Vivian nodded. "Yeah, so I modified things to be more at his level. I told him if he gets *too* cold, he can just knock on the door, and I'll let him back in."

Wade blinked.

"You what?"

"Well, I figured with his age, it wouldn't be the best idea to stay out overnight too often—"

"What planet are you on?"

"Willamond," Vivian replied. "It was the only one I could find in Sector Six currently experiencing an ice age."

Wade cleared his throat. "Vivian..."

"Don't worry, he has plenty of supplies and I helped him build a shelter. He's totally safe. Mostly. This will be his fourth night out there. And it's only two degrees below zero at the coldest temperatures."

Wade looked like he was about to object and then just shook his head. "He's only a child."

"I *know*. I was surprised how resourceful he can be too!"

"I meant..."

"I know what you meant. But the world is hard, Wade. Better for him that it's hard now than later. You said to teach him what I know. I know how to survive."

Wade held up his hands. "Okay, Vivian. Just call me if you need anything.

"I will," Vivian said. Then she added, "And, Wade, stop worrying about what Givon and the Ministry might do. Abigail will be just fine."

2

After two more days out in the cold, Vivian decided Traq had finally had enough.

To be honest, she didn't much like the planet. Willamond was frigid and barren and completely devoid of more than bacterial life. It had been terraformed hundreds of years ago, but during the process, something had gone wrong and the planet had entered an ice age.

They abandoned it, waiting out the frigid temperatures before returning to build settlements. It looked like it was going to be a long and slow process, though, so they would have a long wait.

Traq was starting to impress her with just how tough he was. She'd expected him to come knocking on the ship's door to get warm sometime during the first few nights out there, but he never did. She went to check on him frequently and make sure he was doing all right, but she never actually had to intervene.

His Uncle Jack, it turned out, was the one who was struggling.

"Do you think he's all right?"

"He's fine," Vivian said.

Jack was Traq's uncle, a pilot and soldier for the Republic who was helping her take care of Traq out here in Sector Six. He knew the region and had grown up on Geid, which made him an excellent guide in traveling around the Sector.

But not a great companion.

"I mean, he's been out there all night and you didn't go check on him yet this morning. Do you think I should check on him?"

"He's fine," Vivian said. "We're tracking his vitals. He's still wearing the suit."

"Maybe there was a malfunction and they aren't tracking right."

"There wasn't a malfunction. Traq is fine, just a little cold."

"And lonely."

"Probably."

"I still don't understand why I can't stay out there with him."

"Because he's your nephew. If you go out there with him, then you'll be taking care of him rather than him taking care of himself."

"True, but he's just a kid. He's only seven."

"I know."

"He shouldn't be learning how to survive on his own on an icy planet. He should be learning math and how to have fun and be a kid."

"He is going to get a *full* education, not merely preparatory curriculum. I'm going to prepare him so he's ready to face the world because there are going to be a lot of people who want to find him and use him for their own purposes."

"Why?" Jack asked. "What's so special about him?"

Vivian fell silent and then shook her head. "It's not important right now. Suffice it to say he's different."

"What do you mean by different? What aren't you and Wade telling me?"

Vivian didn't answer. "Do you want to go bring Traq in? We're done with Willamond."

"You mean no more snow training?"

"No. He's finished here."

"Then where to next?"

"Eldun."

"What? Eldun is in the middle of a civil war."

"Exactly. He needs to learn about death and battle."

"He's *seven*."

"You keep saying that. He might be young, but he's also impressionable. Every book I've read says these years are very important for children to learn the most valuable lessons of their lives."

"Still...a war-torn planet? Is that really where you think we should go?"

Vivian hesitated. "Not you," she said. "Me and Traq. You'll be staying on Jaril until we get done."

"What? Why?"

"I need him to understand there is no safety net and he has to be able to take care of himself, and I can't do that if he thinks his uncle will always be here to rescue him. We're only going to be on Eldun for a week, do some hiking and sightseeing of the devastation, and then we'll come pick you up."

Jack frowned at her, but he didn't respond. The conditions around him traveling with her and Traq was that he had to follow her commands; this was one he definitely didn't like.

Vivian could fly the ship without him well enough to get by, so he couldn't push the issue too hard without her simply dismissing him.

But Vivian needed a chance to interact with Traq alone. She'd already mapped out their hiking course on Eldun to make sure they stayed safe. She would dock the ship in the city of Delphi and then take him on a hike to visit the broken cities left in the wake of warfare.

War was still raging on the planet, but thousands of kilometers away from Delphi, so she didn't expect there to be any actual risk. Right now, Delphi was at peace with its neighbors and rebuilding.

That didn't mean it would be completely safe, but she was confident she could protect him during their short venture.

She knew Jack wouldn't like her plan either way, but she didn't plan on giving him any options.

"Only a week?"

"One week of hiking," Vivian agreed. "Just to show him what war looks like so he understands how terrible it is."

"And then you'll come pick me up?"

"Yes. Then we will find somewhere relaxing to hole up for a few years and further his education in mathematics and science. No more dangerous adventures for a long while."

Jack thought about it for a long moment and then nodded. "Okay. If you think this is for the best, then I'm not going to argue."

"I do."

"Then I guess I'd better go gather up Traq."

Jack stood up from his seat in the cockpit and headed farther into the ship, heading for the loading ramp. Vivian watched him go and then leaned back in her chair. Part of her wanted to release the uncle from her services, but she didn't really think she should.

She knew why Argus had sent Jack with her: Argus didn't think she would be capable of raising Traq alone or that maybe she would abandon him along the way. He wasn't Traq's safety net; he was hers. But, it had been two years since she took over caring for Traq, and despite a few misgivings, she'd grown quite attached to him.

Now, Jack was just a burden, and a worrisome one at that. He was always challenging her and second-guessing her. She needed to take that next step in Traq's training and really start pushing him, and that meant separating him from his uncle.

A debate for another day, she decided. She would see how things went on Eldun before deciding if she was ready to send Jack back to Argus and take care of Traq alone.

3

Jack returned a few minutes later with Traq in tow. Traq's cheeks were bright red from the cold and he looked exhausted, but he seemed otherwise all right. He was bundled up in about six layers of brown clothing and looked like a little wooden barrel walking through the ship.

"How do you feel?" Vivian asked.

"Fine," he said. "A little bored."

"Bored is good," Vivian said. "It teaches you how to think and use your imagination."

Traq nodded, but he didn't seem to know quite what he was talking about.

"Am I going back out?" he asked, only the slightest bit of trepidation in his voice.

"No," she said. "We're done here and we're going to be leaving in a short while. This time, we're going somewhere warm to stay for a week."

"Okay."

"Do you want to go get warmed up?" she asked.

He nodded. "Yes, and I'm kind of hungry."

"All right," she said, glancing back at Jack. "Do you want to get him something to eat? I'll prep for takeoff and we can be out of here in about an hour."

"Sure," he said.

He gently took Traq by the shoulder and led him out of the cockpit.

Vivian watched them go and then turned back to the controls. It would only take them a couple of days to drop Jack off and then make it to Eldun.

There was a city outside of Delphi that had been bombed and evacuated in the last few years, and there was no greater way to show the treachery of war than with a city built for millions that was completely destroyed and empty.

To be honest, she was kind of looking forward to it.

Chapter 4
Sector 6 - Jaril
Jim Crater

1

Jim stormed into the little corner bar in the brewery district called the Blue Daisy in a foul mood. He needed a drink to take his mind off of just how bad his life had become. Everything had started to fall apart, and he didn't know just how far things would fall before he hit rock bottom.

Worse, his clothes were uncomfortable and chafed in all of the wrong places. He had *never* worn uncomfortable clothes in his entire life, and it felt like the embodiment of everything else going wrong.

The problem was that they were expensive but worn too often and poorly cared for. Oliver had explained to him that they would need to be taken to expensive establishments for cleaning, but that was something he just didn't have time to do. He hated the way he looked in them because it made him look wrong, like a pretentious rich person.

Oliver had bought them and insisted they would make him appear dignified and that would help keep the people on his side. They were the kind of clothes an Admiral *should* wear, and it would be dangerous to be seen out in public without them. Jim, Oliver explained, had an image to maintain.

They made him feel like he was trying to stand out, though. It was as though he thought he was better than other people, and he hated that. The only part of the outfit he actually liked wearing was the hat.

Of course, that hadn't been a part of Oliver's original outfit. No matter how hard Oliver tried to talk him out of it, he would not get rid of his beloved Safari hat. It helped to hide his thinning hair and he thought it looked dashing on him.

But not even his special occasion hat could cheer him out of his foul mood today. He had thought that once they declared him an Admiral, the Royal Family would solidify his position with the ships and manpower to manage his fleet.

They had lied to him and tricked him, getting what they wanted and leaving him out in the cold. He had never realized how far the corruption had spread in the Royal Family and that they were just using him for their own ends.

Truly, he'd never really understood politics.

Which was why he left that side of things up to Oliver. Honestly, it was the only real reason he kept Oliver around at all. Oliver understood how to deal with people, and he took care of the conversations with the rich and powerful so Jim didn't have to.

For all the good that had done either of them.

Honestly, was it a blessing or a curse that day when Oliver knocked on my door? he wondered.

He was starting to think it might have been a curse. Everything that had happened to him since that fateful day had built him up only to bring him crashing back down to the ground.

"Hello, Jim," a woman greeted him at the counter. Molly, his favorite bartender, but he doubted even she would be able to raise his dampened spirits.

"Molly," he said.

She was a tiny thing with green eyes and dimples on her cheeks. He knew she made good money running the bar in tips, and she was a damned good flirt.

"I wasn't expecting you to step in today," she offered.

"Neither was I," Jim said. "I just needed a break. And a drink."

"Rough day?"

"The worst in a long while," he said. He fished a credit stick out of his pocket and handed it across the counter to her. She plugged it into her data pad.

"What will you be having?"

44

"Something cheap, and a lot of it."

"Coming right up."

Molly poured him a double shot of something amber colored and then poured herself a shot as well. Whiskey, it looked like.

"To rough days," she said, holding up her drink in toast. "At least they keep life interesting."

"You have no idea," Jim said, clinking glasses. He drained the drink and set it back on the counter. "Pour me out three more of those and something from the local tap, if you don't mind."

"Absolutely," Molly replied. She filled a mug with draught beer and then poured out three more shots of the cheap whiskey. Then she grabbed a towel and started wiping down the bar. "You heading to the back?"

"Yeah," he said. "Need some peace and quiet. Is it empty today?"

"Mostly," she said. "Couple people came in earlier. Some dandy, don't know his name, but I haven't seen him in a while. Holler if you need something."

He quickly downed two of the three shots and then headed farther into the Blue Daisy, carrying the last shot and mug with him. The Daisy was located out near the docks, as far from the spaceport or civilization as Jim could get. He didn't like to be seen or recognized, so he liked these quiet and remote destinations.

He headed for one of the back rooms that he preferred. There was a sheet of beads covering the entryway, and it didn't have any windows. He figured he could slip inside, finish his last shot and then nurse his beer for a couple of hours. He hated to admit it, but he was lonely, and he didn't want to get back to the ship until Oliver was finished at his party.

He rounded the corner, pushed through the beads, and then froze, coming face to face with someone he knew all too well.

No.

Can't be.

He wouldn't dare come all the way out here...

"You," he managed to mutter, his voice a mix of shock and anger.

Hektor Menschen, Admiral of the fleet and cousin of the queen, barely acknowledged Jim Crater's statement except to smile on his couch, a glass of whiskey in hand. He raised it in toast to Jim, lips curling into a sadistic smile.

"Me?"

Jim strode across the room to where Hektor sat, towering over the smaller man. The room was empty, except for the two of them, but if Hektor was intimidated, he didn't show it.

Jim felt barely contained anger welling up in his stomach, and his hands were shaking. He put the mug and shot glass on the table and stared at Hektor, clenching and unclenching his fist. Hektor was unfazed.

"Can I order you something?" Hektor asked. "Another drink? Maybe you would prefer something a little bit stronger? I hear this place deals in a large variety of illegal goods, and I've heard all sorts of rumors about the things you...partake in."

"What are you doing here?"

"I wasn't aware that my presence would cause such a stir," Hektor replied, his lips twitching. He dipped a finger into his own glass and stirred the liquid with his finger. Finally, he stuck the finger into his mouth and sucked the liquid off. "I simply came for a drink, not to offend. My sincerest apologies, dear friend."

"Are you here to mock me?"

"I was simply enjoying a refreshment."

"You know this is *my* place."

"Oh, you have a place now?" Hektor asked, no longer smiling. "Good that you know it is not with my family."

"You aren't allowed here."

"I am allowed *anywhere*," Hektor replied icily.

Hektor didn't fit in at the Blue Daisy at all. *Pompous* was an apt descriptor. Oliver referred to Hektor as a pretentious *fop*. Whereas Jim's hair was short and unkempt, Hektor's was long and colored silver. He pulled it back into a tight ponytail, every hair perfectly sculpted into position. He had a precise mustache on his lip that matched his hair through use of expensive dyes.

Jim Crater let out a shuddering breath. "You wouldn't be caught dead in here without a good reason. Which means you are here because of me."

"Perhaps I am."

"Why?"

"To see you hiding out here for myself. Why do you attempt to remain out of the spotlight? I've known about this place for some time. It's sad, really. Are you so afraid of your own influence?"

"Maybe I'm scared of what I might do if I run into you in a public place."

"You don't intimidate me," Hektor said airily, sipping his drink. "And you certainly wouldn't risk killing me. I am above you in station and in quality."

Jim Crater was certain that if he broke a wooden beam over the pretentious man's head, he still wouldn't find a single hair out of place.

If nothing else, he was willing to try.

"Not here," Jim corrected. "With what I have in mind for you, death would be a mercy."

"Strong words from such a weak man. Are you willing to back them up?" Hektor asked.

"Weighing the pros and cons," Jim Crater said.

He bit back his anger. He knew Hektor was goading him and trying to provoke a response. Any confrontation wouldn't end well for Jim, so the best thing he could do was get his rage under control. He forced down a few steadying breaths.

"I didn't come here *only* to mock you," Hektor said. "And I know you will never willingly offer yourself up to corporeal punishment over a brawl, even with me. You aren't an utter buffoon."

"I wish I could say the same."

"I just came to deliver a message from my cousin the King. Your term as Admiral is nearly up, and they are considering whether to continue allowing you to remain in the position."

"Admirals serve for life."

"You don't. They can't kick you out of the family, but you are an embarrassment without a fleet. They will remove you shortly and mark you down as a stain in history."

Jim felt a lump get caught in his throat. Those were absolutely *not* the terms of his position when he was first given the title, but he'd been expecting this conversation for a while. He knew Hektor was actively working to remove him from his position.

Expecting the conversation, however, didn't make it any easier to deal with when it came about.

"Of course," Jim said, refusing to show any of his trepidation.

"You have exactly one week before time runs out. Enjoy it while it lasts."

Jim Crater clenched his jaw. "And you're so sure what that decision will be? They would scrap thousands of years of history to make me the first Admiral to be removed from his position while still alive?"

"Oh no," Hektor replied smoothly. "I never said anything about you remaining alive. As you said, Admirals can only leave the position one way."

Jim hesitated. He didn't know if Hektor meant they would publicly execute him or assassinate him. He supposed that in the end, it didn't really matter: whatever the Royal Family decided would happen either way.

"In any case, I just wanted to make sure you were aware that you would only have one more week to enjoy the perks this life has offered you."

With that, Hektor drained his glass of whiskey and set it on the counter. He wiped his mouth and smiled at Jim before speaking again.

"You know, here I was worrying all day about the meeting between you and Lady Margaret Cortet. My sweet little sister told me you'd been invited to a banquet by the family, but somehow I just *knew* you wouldn't attend. Even trained monkeys dislike wearing costumes."

He flashed Crater a final smile, dropped a few credits onto the table, and disappeared through the beads toward the front of the bar. He was whistling, and the sound ripped into Jim's skull. Crater stood there, struggling to maintain his composure. Suddenly he needed to punch something.

2

Jim was fuming as he stormed through the Davenport Market, heading toward the wealthy district on the other side of the city. "Those lazy good for nothing..." he mumbled absently, talking about no one in particular.

His senses were assaulted on all sides by myriad sights, sounds, and smells of the marketplace. He barely noticed any of it as he strode past outdoor kiosks where merchants were peddling a variety of goods, weaving through the crowd and bumping into pedestrians as he went.

One man was selling a bucketful of silver eels writhing over one another like snakes. They were delicious when stewed with peppers, but their small bones could be a choking hazard if prepared improperly.

Another man sold small green pastries made of a sweet and sour fruit, and a small woman ran alongside passersby hoping to find customers for her collection of holdout pistols. She didn't seem to recognize Jim as an Admiral, but she did sense his foul mood enough to at least steer clear of him.

He was grateful.

This was the only place in the city that still attempted to foster human interaction. Most transactions were handled digitally and rarely in person. This market was modeled after the fish markets on Geid and was always loud and boisterous. Many people loved it.

But Jim, on the other hand, had actually been to Geid. He knew of the poverty and devastation those people faced to keep food on the tables of the nobility living here. It disgusted him watching well-dressed and rich citizens wandering through this outdoor market and pretending to understand.

These people were born into money and hadn't worked a day in their lives. They thought this market was meant to honor the people of Geid, but all it did was make a mockery of them.

Jim passed through the market and onto one of the side streets, heading toward a district of expensive mansions. Oliver had been right: It was a beautiful day in the city, which was rare this time of year. The weather was cold at best and usually snowing this late in the season.

He needed to find Oliver. All of the accounts were in both of their names, and Jim needed Oliver to withdraw all of his funds. He would take whatever money he had left and leave the Indeil Kingdom for Terminus and the Republic beyond.

It was a painful decision, but it would spare him the embarrassment of losing his status. He'd given his entire life over to the Kingdom, first in his years of service in the Royal Navy, then as a private citizen, and now as an Admiral, and he would be damned if he would stick around to watch them take it all away.

Maybe he could work as a trade liaison for Oliver and their booming business. He knew that Oliver would have no issue sticking around in the Kingdom: he'd never been raised to the same status as Jim, and he was better at fitting in and not getting squashed by the powerful people.

Especially when there was money to be made. Maybe Jim could serve as a contact to help build their business and make a fortune. It would be of slim value compared to his dream of being an Admiral, but it was better than nothing.

It would be better for Oliver, too, when he really thought about it. Oliver had managed to use their new circumstances to make a small fortune. Without Jim getting in the way, it would be easier to leverage his fame for even more wealth and power.

"Out of my way," Jim growled, pushing his way through the crowd.

He would go to the silly party and find Oliver, withdraw his funds, and then leave. He could see the writing on the walls. Right now all he cared about was getting out of the Kingdom before Hektor could find him and lob more insults his direction.

Or worse, before he followed through with his promise and murdered Jim.

Chapter 5
Sector 4 – Tellus
Maven Ophidian

1

Maven leaned against one of the pillars in the gaudy throne room Darius had set up, listening to her sister Alyssa and Darius argue and bicker like a couple of angry schoolchildren. They didn't have a clear goal about what they were trying to accomplish and kept making ignorant decisions, and Maven was starting to get tired of it.

The problem was they were allied against her and she was voted down at every turn. Darius had declared himself a leader of this little rebellion because he was the first to turn against the Ministry and flee.

But, when she really got down to it, Darius was just an ignorant braggart in way over his head. He didn't know strategy well enough to actually make any headway against the Republic, nor could he make any of his actions count. Killing Captain Lyle Questan, for example, could have been the sort of thing that they turned into an advantage for their side.

Instead, it had been nearly two years and everyone had forgotten about it. Worse, it meant that no other Captain would risk turning against the Republic. Darius's arrogance had cost them a steady source of new recruits.

Right now, the pair were standing up on top of the raised platform in the throne room, shouting and gesticulating their arms wildly at each other as they argued about the best course for their rebellion to take: Alyssa wanted to do *something,* even if it got their fleet destroyed, and Darius was trying to counsel her to be patient.

Maven hated this room as much as Darius loved it. The long hallway leading up to the pedestal, the sheer expense and gravity of the throne, it all just annoyed her. Darius thought it made him look like a powerful leader, but it did exactly the opposite: it made him look like he was just a pretender.

Real leaders didn't need affectation or theatrics to get their point across.

Of course, she had to admit a touch of hypocrisy in her own situation. She knew her breathing mask and robes intimidated people, as well as the stories and rumors about the disfigurement she'd experienced as a child.

She'd helped perpetuate those rumors and exaggerated the situation, but she wasn't doing it *only* to intimidate people. She did it because showing people the real scars or wounds she carried could never live up to what their imaginations could create.

"We need to stop wasting resources," Alyssa shouted, catching Maven's attention and drawing her out of her thoughts. "We need to stop trying to win the hearts and minds of the Indeil Kingdom and win their loyalty instead!"

Maven glanced up at them and saw that Darius had sat down on his throne and was trying to calm Alyssa down. Trying...and failing. Right now she looked much like a ravenous animal standing in front of Darius. Maven folded her arms across her chest and watched the show unfold.

"Do you understand how many ships we could get if we turned them to our side? How many soldiers?" Darius asked. "If we win them over, we get *all* of them."

"We already tried," Alyssa said, casting a sidelong glance at Maven. "And failed."

They were talking about the unallied Kingdom of Sector Six, and Alyssa was making sure to remind everyone that it was Maven's failure that kept the Sector from joining their rebellion.

That was, at least, Alyssa's interpretation of what happened, but not the reality. The original plan had been shortsighted and reckless, intending to scare Jaril into joining with force and brutality. Alyssa had been insistent that an overwhelming show of force would win them over.

She thought of Jaril and the Indeil Kingdom as hopeless peasants who only understood violence, and they would have to crack a few eggs to bring them into the fold. She was ready to kill half of them if it meant the other half would serve her.

The problem was, the exact opposite situation was the reality. Just because Sector Six was a long way from the Core worlds didn't mean it was backward. The people there were well educated and independent, and a show of violence would only increase their loyalty to the crown. They would fight to the death against Darius and his army, which would end up costing them everything.

Alyssa's plan was doomed to fail from the outset, yet Maven had been forced to prove it to Darius; he wouldn't take her at her word. She'd taken a fleet to the Kingdom, installed a blockade, and attempted to negotiate with the Royal Family. Not even a week had passed before they turned against her and attacked.

"Maven should have attacked," Alyssa said, addressing Darius but staring at Maven. "She had an entire fleet to command. She could have broken their will in a day."

"It wouldn't have worked," Maven replied.

"We had every advantage on our side. They were wholly unprepared for an engagement. You could have crippled them and forced their submission."

"Then we would have spent every waking hour watching our backs and wondering when they would seek their revenge. What happens when they turn against us in the middle of a large conflict against the Republic?"

"Then we teach them another lesson."

Maven could only shake her head in response, wondering why she'd ended up with such an ignorant woman for her twin sister. Alyssa was violent and angry and knew nothing about how people functioned.

Which made sense, considering she grew up in the Ministry. It was a violent and shady organization masquerading as a religious institution. Everything Alyssa had learned about dominating and breaking people she'd learned honestly.

Still, it would have been nice to have a sister who transcended the ignorant brutality of her childhood. They would be able to accomplish so much more together. Instead, they were very nearly enemies.

"We need to try again," Darius replied. "There's nowhere else in the galaxy we can turn to for even *half* as many troops and ships to supplement our fleet."

"Sector Two," Alyssa argued. "Peter Gavriel hates the First Citizen as much as we hate the Ministry. He will join us in a heartbeat. He would bring ships, money, power, and legitimacy to the Union."

"He would never *join* us," Darius replied. "He would hijack the Union from us and use it for his own goals. At best, he would sacrifice everything we've built to further his own goals, and at worst, he would betray us to give himself a leg up in his own dealings. Either way, it would cost us everything."

"It would at least be a step in the right direction."

"What direction is that?"

"Destroying the Republic."

"What good will that do us if we just replace it with something worse? No, we aren't ready for that confrontation yet. We need more ships before we can take that step. When we approach the Consul, we need to offer him an *equal* partnership with what we've already built, which means we need our own fleet that can at least come close to rivaling his."

"We need more than that," Maven spoke up. They fell silent, glancing down the steps at her. Darius frowned at her, and Alyssa just looked annoyed that she was interrupting their discussion.

"What do you mean?"

"Peter Gavriel hates the First Citizen, but his people—the people of Sector Two—love the Republic. Sure, there are some that would cherish an opportunity to break free of the taxes and bureaucracy, but by and large they are happy with what they have."

"Whatever the Consul decides to do, the people will follow" Darius replied, standing up from his chair and looking down at her. "If Peter declares his intention to join our Union, then the other planets will have no choice but to follow his lead."

"You're looking at it backward," Maven replied. "Whatever the *people* decide to do, Peter will have no choice but to follow...*if* he wants to remain in charge."

"That's silly," Alyssa said. "You're suggesting the people would overthrow him if they didn't like his choices?"

"In a heartbeat," Maven said. "The people have no love for him, and they have no real desire for war or rebellion. But...if we give them a reason..."

Darius was silent for a moment, scratching his chin and thinking. Maven hated waiting for him to make up his mind like this, but she knew better than to interrupt him. He had quite the temper. Finally, he turned to face her.

"What do you have in mind?"

Maven stepped away from the pillar she was leaning against and walked toward the center of the room. The only sound in the great hall was her breathing mask.

She took a few seconds to savor the look of seething rage on her sister's face. Alyssa hated when Darius took Maven seriously because it weakened her hold over him. She hated the idea that he could have thoughts of his own.

"First, we focus on Daer."

"Why Daer?"

"Daer is full of cutthroats and bandits and all kinds of unsavory individuals. They have no love for the Republic, but they won't love our Union either. Their only love is profit. Offer them that and they will seek to join us."

"Offer them money? That won't be enough to win them over."

"No, it won't, but it's a start. Plus, they already have incentive to want to leave the Republic after what Captain Grove did two years ago. They have long memories and won't soon forget the culling."

"Peter Gavriel won't listen if the seediest planet in his Sector wants to join us."

"No," Maven agreed. "But if Regamon *and* Daer want to join our Union, the Consul will have to seriously consider his options if he wants to remain in control of Sector Two. At that point, any deal you offer him he'll accept, including an equal or lesser partnership."

"Why would Regamon want to join us?" Alyssa asked. "They are the richest planet in the Republic and almost rival Axis in power. They are all rich, fat, and happy with their lot in life."

Maven smiled, though she knew they couldn't see it behind her mask. "Trust me, by the time I'm done with them, they'll be begging to join us."

Darius rubbed his white goatee. "What would you need?"

"You can't seriously be listening to this?" Alyssa argued, grabbing Darius by the shoulder. He brushed her off, ignoring her.

"Identities in the Sector," Maven said. "Four of them, and they need to be perfect and untraceable."

"That's not going to be easy," Darius replied. "I'll have to call in a lot of favors to get something like that."

"It'll be worth it."

"You just want to put your little toy soldiers on Regamon," Alyssa said, shaking her head. "But they haven't been very effective yet, have they? You've had two years of this little charade with the Academy and what have you accomplished?"

"We have turned three planets to the Union and crippled the economies of four other planets."

"And, in the grand scheme of things, that is almost nothing."

"So far we've only sent out new recruits to smaller planets to test the waters," Maven argued. "We haven't tried something on this scale before."

"Why would we assume this is anything different?"

"This is the first group of recruits, and they have been training for this mission for the last two years," Maven replied. "I trust you remember them well?"

Alyssa's expression turned dark. A few years earlier Alyssa had gone to the Silvent Academy to ruin her sister's plans, but she'd managed to get herself kidnapped by Jayson and his crew instead.

Maven had never let her live it down.

"We should have executed them."

Maven shrugged. "Or given them medals."

"What is your plan?" Darius asked, ignoring the banter.

"To sow dissent in the region. We can infiltrate and invade their systems of government and turn the planet against the Republic."

"You think you can do this? We don't have a lot of resources near the Core worlds, and if I burn them for nothing, it could severely cripple us."

"I know I can," Maven said. "Trust me."

"Like we trusted you before?" Alyssa asked. "You promised us you could take Sector Six, and it's been two years and it still isn't ours."

"I never promised anything, and it was your preposterous theory that crippled our efforts there anyway."

56

"You had an *armada*. You could have taken the planet by force in an afternoon."

"Should I have attacked them and destroyed the very fleet we were there to acquire? The cost would have been too high. Taking Jaril by force would serve us no purpose. We need for them to follow us willingly, which means we need for them to *join* us willingly."

"We could execute the ones who aren't loyal."

"Like we did with Captain Lyle's fleet? We lost over half of the soldiers and are still short of fully manning *any* of the ships. No, we need for the Royal Family to join us willingly and bring their entire fleet as allies, and building something like that takes time."

"Too much time."

"I will turn them to our cause within a few years. If you are so intent on promises, then you can have one for this. I promise to gain their loyalty, but I will do it *my* way. The same as turning Regamon, which means you need to trust me."

Alyssa pursed her lips. "Our patience is wearing thin," she said, turning to Darius. "We should deploy another fleet to Jaril, and this time put someone more suited to the task in charge of winning the Kingdom. We *can* take Jaril, and when we do, their entire fleet will all fall into line."

Maven bristled at the words and nearly lashed out at her sister. All three of them had begun this rebellion together, yet Alyssa seemed to think she held a higher station than her twin sister.

Maven forced herself to control the anger and took a deep breath. She didn't need to have it out with Alyssa. Not here. It was the wrong time and place, so she simply filed the insult away in her memories for when she finally paid her sister back in full.

"I will take the Sector *my* way," Maven said slowly. "They will join us willingly. All of their ships and soldiers *will* fight for us, and I won't need to kill a single one of them to do it."

Darius stared at her for a long while before finally nodding.

"Fine," he said, waving his hand in dismissal. "We won't deploy a fleet...yet. But we need to see some results, Maven. You can't keep everything to yourself. I'll give you the resources to send your soldiers to Sector Two, and you give us some results."

Maven nodded. She assumed the conversation was over and started to leave, but then Alyssa spoke up.

"What about that research center on Alderson?"

She spun. "What about it?"

"You said you were looking into it. That was the only reason we let you reopen your stupid Academy anyway. We need the research that they were working on before the Republic abandoned it."

Darius nodded. "Yes. You said it would contain information about genetically engineering the perfect soldiers. Have you recovered it yet?"

Maven hesitated. The research facility on Alderson had no doubt contained information about the Fists of the First Citizen, but that had been years ago. She was sure that all of it had been destroyed when the facility was abandoned years earlier.

Which meant that sending in recruits to clear it out was a waste of time and resources. But that *had* been one of the primary reasons Darius had given her the Academy, and he was expecting some sort of explanation for why it was still abandoned.

"It's been overrun with wildlife and creatures. We sent some recruits in to clean it up, but they didn't return."

"Because of some animals?" Alyssa asked incredulously. "Did the rabbits give them trouble?"

"The Republic chose Alderson for the Silvent Academy specifically because it was dangerous," Maven replied. "There are a lot of hostile elements native to Alderson, including unforgivable climates and dangerous predators."

"So...where is the problem?"

Maven didn't respond. She turned to Darius instead. "We can, of course, clear the facility out if you give me a few hundred soldiers. Any research that was left behind will be brought here within two months' time."

Darius hesitated and then shrugged. "Sure. I'll dispatch a ship to go clear out the wildlife and—"

"Why soldiers?" Alyssa interrupted. "Why not have someone else take care of it?"

"What do you mean?"

"Well, Maven wants you to put *our* assets on the line for her little pet soldiers. Why not have them take care of this problem as well?"

"They are spies, not soldiers," Maven argued.

"They've been training to fight, have they not?" Alyssa asked. "You assured us that by the time they were ready, they would be the best soldiers and infiltrators we had at our disposal. Here's your chance to prove it."

"We need them for the mission to Regamon," Maven replied. "We can't risk them for something foolish like this."

"On the contrary, we can't risk *our* assets in the Core on unproven resources. You said yourself that they hadn't been out in the field. From everything you've told us, these soldiers should be able to handle a situation like this easily. This will give them an opportunity to prove it before risking everything for them."

"And if they die?"

"Then we shouldn't have sent them to Regamon anyway, right? Are you saying your little toy soldiers aren't up for the job?"

Maven hesitated. She knew she was in a rough position because from everything she'd heard from Alexander Robertson at the Silvent Academy, the creatures that had overtaken the research facility weren't to be trifled with.

But she couldn't risk looking weak or admitting that her infiltrators weren't ready for Regamon.

"Of course, they can handle it. They are very resourceful. They could handle a situation like this unarmed, if need be."

"Excellent," Alyssa said, turning to Darius. "Then this should be a rather good test for them. We can make a game of it, if you like?"

"What do you mean?" he asked.

"We will send them in with no weapons or armor and tell them nothing about what they are to face. Then, we will see just how resourceful they really are. Once they handle this situation, we can be satisfied that they are worthy of calling in favors and planting them in Sector Two."

"We're playing games with their lives? We should send them in armed," Maven argued.

"*You* said they didn't need weapons. They are quite resourceful, are they not?"

"'Resourceful' isn't the same thing as 'magical.' We should—"

"You don't think they can handle it?" Darius interrupted, rubbing his goatee.

"Of course they can," Maven said.

Darius nodded. "Then it sounds like a solid idea and the perfect way to test their training. We can have soldiers on standby to rescue them should things get out of hand, but let's see if they can take care of it alone, first."

"A wager," Alyssa offered. "If you win and they survive, then we will give you anything you need to send them to Regamon."

"And if they die?"

"Then, we send a fleet to Jaril and take the planet by force and ignore all of this foolishness."

Maven looked at Darius, but he didn't seem interested in getting involved. She hated Alyssa more in that moment than any other time in her life. She was petty and stupid but manipulative as hell.

"Fine," she said. "Deal."

"Should we shake on it?"

"Don't push your luck."

"It's settled then," Darius said. "Let us know when the research facility is taken care of, Maven."

"Of course," Maven said, stifling a groan.

"I'll be there in a few days," Alyssa said, smiling at her sister. "To make sure that the full terms of our wager are carried out. We wouldn't want any cheating to take place, would we?"

Maven turned on her heels and stormed out of the throne room before they could stop her again. She was furious with her sister and needed to blow off some steam.

She was also furious with herself for walking into her sister's trap. Alyssa might be ignorant about a lot of things, but she was incredibly manipulative and good at getting her own way.

Now, everything was riding on her four recruits: Jayson, Richard, Brett, and Tricia. If they were successful in this upcoming venture, then she would be in the perfect position to accomplish many of her plans.

However, if they died in that facility...

Well, she needed to be certain that didn't happen.

She had no doubt that her assets—these four that had survived from the original seven—could handle cleaning up the facility, but if any of them were compromised during the mission, she would never forgive her sister.

2

Maven, once she was safely back in her own sealed chambers, removed her breathing mask and went to her terminal to contact Alexander Robertson. She was still angry, but now her mind was sifting through possibilities to get everything done as safely and efficiently as possible.

He connected almost immediately, looking concerned.

"Is everything all right?" he asked.

"Mostly," she said. "Only minor setbacks."

Alexander was a kindly looking old man in his late seventies. He walked with a cane and had flowing white hair and a beard, but she knew most of it was for show and he was deadly in a fight. He wanted people to underestimate him so he could use their sympathies against them.

Much the same as herself.

"The mission will go off as intended, but there's been a hiccup in the plans."

"What do you mean?"

"Darius wants the research facility to be cleared."

"He's sending troops?"

"Not exactly," Maven replied. "He wants the four to do it."

"Risky."

"Not my plan," she said, "but Alyssa is still harboring a grudge. Soldiers will be on standby, but are not to interfere unless necessary."

"That won't do any good," he said. "By the time they have to intervene, they will all be dead."

"I know. But there is no alternative."

"Should I give Jayson the armor to use?"

"No," Maven said. "You can't tell them of what they will find inside either."

"The Wyrms?"

"They can't know. This test is to see how well they can handle a situation they are wholly unprepared for."

Alexander rubbed his chin. "Dangerous, yet it *is* a good way to test them."

"Alyssa wants to test their resourcefulness. We're to send them in unarmed and unprepared to deal with this threat and see how they handle themselves."

"Unarmed? That is suicide."

"I know," Maven said. "But those were the terms of the wager to place them in Sector Two."

"What do we do when they fail?"

"They can't fail," she replied. "I can't risk losing this opportunity. Everything hinges on their success in this endeavor. *Denigen's Fist* will be patrolling Sector Two in a few months, and we need to make this happen while Captain Grove is near Regamon. This little hiccup could cost me years of planning."

"Maybe you should just tell Darius what you intend."

"Alyssa would sabotage my plans if she caught wind of them. She's desperate to see me fail, even at the cost of her own rebellion."

"Then what do we do?"

"Bend the rules," Maven replied. "Alyssa will be arriving in a few days to monitor the situation. Get them out of the Academy and away from her. I don't care what it takes, but they must succeed at this mission and clear out the facility. Don't let her know what you are doing, but see to it that things go according to plan."

"And then what?"

"And then get them ready to go to Regamon as soon as they are recovered."

"I'll do my best."

"Yes, you will. Do it as though your life depends on it."

She ended the connection before Alexander could respond, satisfied she'd gotten her point across. She wasn't sure if she would kill Alexander or not if he failed, and if anything that was a problem for another day.

She did know, however, that all of her careful planning and manipulation would be for naught if they didn't survive this mission. She'd spent years forming her alliances in Sector Six and planning this mission in Sector Two, and she would lose all of it if this didn't work.

She had a lot of things juggling in the air right now, plans in motion. It was like a house of cards, and if even one fell out of place, then her entire castle might come crumbling down around her.

Still, if she *was* successful in fracturing the Republic, and if she managed to turn Sector Six to their cause, then they would have a serious chance at toppling the Republic and building their own government from out of its ashes. She would be in a much stronger position than she was today, closer to finally ripping control of the Union from Darius and Alyssa.

She'd never been so close to achieving her goals before.

Chapter 6

Sector 6 – Axis
Abdullah Al Hakir

1

Abdullah sat in the common eating area where enlisted men took their meals, down in the belly of the beast. He was sitting arm to arm with men well below his rank and station aboard the Capital Class warship *Denigen's Fist*.

He knew the Captain frowned on him coming down here to eat and mingle amidst the crew, but it was one of the few things he refused to give up from his old life before his promotion to First Officer. His life might have changed in every other way, but at least once in a while, he wanted to pretend like he was still an average soldier.

Actually, he came down here far less than he'd originally planned: When he was promoted to First Officer, he'd committed to taking all of his meals with the enlisted soldiers. It made sense to him to spend time with the men and women he was in charge of because it felt like the right way to build connections with his soldiers and bridge the leadership gap he was so used to. He didn't want to be unapproachable and aloof like all of the other officers.

He wanted to be better: an enigma to the crew that they could look up to. He wanted for them to know that he didn't think he was above them and that he was here to look after their wellbeing.

Jamir Paskin, Captain Groves' personal assistant, had warned him against such action. He said that rather than it making him personable, the crew would feel that he was accountable. They would demand and beg and plead, and it was important for them to know that there *was* a gap and difference between them. Jamir told him that it was important for the crew to know that he *was* above them in station.

But Abdullah had ignored the advice.

Taking all of his meals down here in the mess hall in the belly of the beast, however, was a goal he quickly abandoned. The reality of his new position set in, and the novelty of the situation wore off. It wasn't only the fact that his new job kept him tremendously busy and it was easier to take his meals alone, it was also how many problems were brought to his attention when he was in the mess.

Jamir had been right. Every little issue soldiers had aboard the ship, every little quirk or problem that had *nothing* to do with Abdullah's new position, was brought up. The soldiers would beg, plead, or even demand that he fix the problem. They felt like Abdullah owed them something.

They didn't take his willingness to eat with them as a sign of his affection for them: They took it as a taunt, like he was mocking them. Nothing could have been further from the truth, but he couldn't convince them of that.

He hadn't minded hearing about their problems even, at least to an extent. He truly wanted to help fix them; it was simply the sheer number and frequency of the grievances. The soldiers came to him in floods while he was trying to eat and laid out their issues.

He needed a filter for it all, something to make the problems more manageable. Every single little issue that they had with him or any other officer came to him, and it became a source for them to vent their frustrations. He had simply become overwhelmed with it and was forced to abandon his lofty ambitions.

So, he stopped eating in the belly of the beast and began taking his meals in the officer's mess hall, but that was just as bad if not worse. The officers were pigs and elitists who felt they were better than the enlisted soldiers simply because of their status outside of the military and the rich and powerful families they came from.

They hated Abdullah, and it felt like being in school all over again. He often ate alone or with Eddie. He hated those officers for their unwillingness to even try to see the world from someone else's perspective.

It was mutual, however, in that they hated Abdullah just as much as he hated them. In the last two years since he'd been raised to the rank of First Officer, they had never forgiven him, and he doubted they ever would. They felt like he was an imposter, pretending at his new role, and that it wouldn't last.

Maybe they were right.

So, he took all of his meals now in his private quarters, but still once a month he bit the bullet and came down to eat in the mess hall with the enlisted soldiers. He might have abandoned part of his ambition in the face of his new reality, but there were some ideals he still clung to.

2

"How is it?" Eddie Boleman asked, interrupting him from his thoughts. Abdullah looked blankly at his friend. "The food, how is it?"

In response, Abdullah held up his spoon, letting greasy and disgusting bean-based paste roll off of it to slop back onto his tray. The tray was a flat slab of plastic with four little raised sections to hold separate pastes, much like a prison tray. The soldiers often joked that at least in prison their meals would contain some semblance of real food.

"It's as good as I remember," he muttered.

Part of him was actually a little upset with himself. Now that he was important aboard the ship, his meals were cooked by a professional chef and made of only the finest ingredients. He had access to foods and beverages that enlisted soldiers could only dream of. Eating this...food...in the mess hall had never been a problem for him before being promoted, so why was it suddenly so disgusting for him?

At some point, he'd become a snob.

"Better, if you ask me," Eddie said. "They actual use a few real spices now."

"Do they? Yeah, I guess I can taste a little...cumin?"

"The Captain promised change," Eddie said, smirking. "Do you think this is what she meant?"

Eddie Boleman was one of Abdullah's oldest friends, an attractive man with curly golden hair and a winning smile. He came from a rich family and had no reason to join the military except as a rebellion against his parents and their goals for him.

He could have been an officer, and an important one at that, just by the weight of his name. He came from an important family that served the Republic on Regamon. But he'd elected to enlist directly instead and earn everything on his own. He was one of the least pretentious rich people that Abdullah had ever known.

After his promotion to First Officer, Abdullah had pulled Eddie and a few other soldiers up and made them his advisors and important Officers in their own right. He could have picked anyone, but he wanted to keep his friends as close as possible.

Unlike Abdullah, Eddie looked every bit the part he was playing as an Officer aboard *Denigen's Fist*, with his uniform accentuating all of his features and making him look even more distinguished. Somehow, he always managed to press his uniform as well, something Abdullah had never managed to get right.

The thing that Abdullah loved about Eddie was that he was the only one of his advisors who would come down here with him once a month to eat with the other soldiers. The rest refused to even set foot in the mess hall, but Eddie had no problem bumping elbows with people beneath his station. After all, they used to live down here, too.

It wasn't the only thing he loved about Eddie, but it helped. Abdullah had been romantically in love with Eddie for more years than he could count, long before his promotion, but so far he'd never managed to admit his feelings to the other man. He was terrified of what sort of response he might receive in return, and he was afraid he might lose their friendship if he asked for something more.

"I hear we're going to Sector Two in a couple of months," Eddie said, taking a bite of his own slop.

"Patrolling," Abdullah replied, nodding. He looked at his food and decided he just couldn't stomach it right now. Just thinking about it made him feel sick. He would have some food sent to his quarters once he left here.

"We haven't gone out there in a long time," Eddie said. "Not since..."

"I know. Not since Daer."

"Do you think...?"

"No. We aren't actually going anywhere near Daer. Regamon is our main priority, and it hasn't had any real problems in years."

"That's good," Eddie said. "We could use some downtime."

"Speaking of which," Abdullah said, "we're going to have some leave time on Regamon. All of my officers and advisors are getting two weeks off to just kick back and relax."

"No way? Do you think I'll be able to go see my family?"

"That's why I requested it," Abdullah said. "I figured if we were all going to get some time off, I might as well make it at the best time for you to see your parents."

"That's awesome, man. I'll have to send my mom a message and let her know I'll be coming to visit. She's going to be crazy excited. You'll come with me, right? To meet them? They'll love you."

Abdullah tried not to read too much into the statement, or to blush, and nodded. "Sure. I'll be able to stop over."

He doubted, though, that they would love him. Eddie came from an old-fashioned family that believed their station in life was a God-given right because they were better than everyone else. The Ministry taught that people received benefits based on their merit, so naturally, being born into a rich family meant you were better than the rest.

But, he wasn't about to point out to Eddie that idea. At the very least, he knew that they would be polite enough to tolerate him, considering his station aboard *Denigen's Fist*. But he knew better than to think they would ever like him.

"That's awesome. A real vacation. We haven't had one of those since you got promoted."

"I know, but we'll get one soon. I promise."

Eddie smiled. "Best news I've had in weeks."

"We'll be able to do anything you want once we get there, but if you are interested, I was wondering if..."

He trailed off, noticing a commotion on the far side of the mess hall. A group of soldiers had gathered, and he heard shouts and raised voices. It looked like they were forming up into a circle, which could never be a good thing.

Eddie glanced over as well, and they climbed off of the benches, heading in that direction to see what was happening. By the time they got there, the shouting had escalated and people were starting to shove each other.

It was quickly turning violent and getting out of hand, and it looked like whatever had happened was on the verge of bursting into an all-out brawl. He exchanged a glance with Eddie and tried to make his way through the crowd.

"What is the meaning of this?" he shouted, pushing his way between a pair of men. They ignored him and kept shoving each other, shouting and gesticulating wildly. "What's going on?"

They continued ignoring him. He tried raising his voice to get their attention, but no one seemed interested in paying him any mind.

"Officer on deck!" Eddie roared next to him, grabbing a man and shoving him forward into the center of the ring. He stepped forward next to him, turning and eyeing the gathered soldiers around them.

Everyone froze, turning to look at Abdullah. In an instant, all of the soldiers drew back, standing at attention and with frightened expressions on their faces.

In the center of the ring sat a half-naked girl, crying and holding up scraps of clothing to cover herself.

"What is the meaning of this?" Abdullah asked, addressing no one in particular.

"She ran here, sir," one soldier said. "She was raped, and her attacker threatened to kill her."

"She wasn't raped," another soldier shouted, stepping forward. Two men grabbed him and dragged him back. "She's lying!"

The first soldier nodded toward the man. "He is the accused."

Abdullah frowned and turned to Eddie. "Get her to medical and take him to the brig."

"I'm innocent!" the man shouted again. "That lying—"

Eddie drew his pistol and aimed it at the man's face.

"Say one more word and I'll end you right now," he said, voice low and calm.

The man fell silent, and Eddie slipped his gun away. Abdullah winced as he looked at his friend, dismayed. On the one hand, he felt that what Eddie had done was maybe something *he* should have done, but on the other hand it wasn't acceptable behavior from any officer, let alone one who served under him.

They should never draw their guns unless they intended to use them. That was a lesson he'd learned from his Captain.

He would need to reprimand Eddie for it later, but for now, he decided to let it slide. The last thing he intended to do was reprimand Eddie in front of the other soldiers, especially when all Eddie was doing was trying to help.

"Take care of this and get her to the med-bay. I'm going to go speak with the Captain."

"Do you want a rape kit?"

"Yes," he said. "And a full report on exactly what happened. We need to get to the bottom of this."

3

"Captain, I—"

"I heard," Captain Grove interrupted. Abdullah was walking onto the bridge aboard *Denigen's Fist*, and he could tell that Captain Grove was waiting for him. She stood near the viewport, watching the doorway with a pensive expression on her face. "The reports came through only moments ago from the med-bay. The girl is being examined, but it looks like she was telling the truth."

"So, she was raped?"

"It is likely."

Abdullah could hardly believe that. In his entire time aboard the ship, he'd rarely heard of any crimes being committed, let alone something so severe. Certainly, in the last few years no one had been willing to do anything like that, not after the Passing of Command ceremony.

They knew Captain Grove wasn't likely to forgive.

"The man maintains his innocence."

"His DNA was found on her. He is surely guilty."

"What will be done with him?"

"That is for you to decide," the Captain replied.

Abdullah froze. "Me?"

"Yes," she said. "This is the first time something like this has happened since you were made First Officer. You need to decide how we will proceed, and your word will be the law in this matter."

"You want me to decide his punishment?"

She nodded. "You have complete control over the situation and can utilize whatever resources you wish in making your decision. Though, forensics won't be tremendously necessary, as it looks very cut and dry."

"What should I do? Should I execute him?"

She shook her head. "This is your decision, not mine. I will await your answer."

She turned away from him and began speaking to another officer, dismissing him. He stared at her, the weight of what she had just told him sinking in.

He'd never imagined making a decision like this. He'd expected to bring the matter to the Captain's attention and let her deal with it. After all, she was the Captain and had complete control over her crew.

She was allowed to delegate matters to her officers, of course, he just hadn't expected her to. Especially not for something like this. The idea that he would have to decide this man's fate, and worse what his punishment would be for the crime, was unthinkable.

Head spinning, Abdullah bowed to his Captain, turned around, and strode back off the bridge.

Chapter 7
Sector 4 – Alderson
Jayson Coley

1

"Another group is leaving," Jayson said. "Tomorrow, from the sounds of it. They're going off world."

He was sitting in the crowded mess hall of the Silvent Academy along with Richard and Tricia. It was the midday meal, so the entire place was filled with the conversations and shouting of the boisterous new recruits that had shown up over the last two years.

His chest had healed up in the last few days, but it still hurt when he breathed too deeply. It was the first time he'd ever been shot, and there was a new scar on his chest where the armor had cut him as a memento of it.

The Academy was completely different than when they'd first arrived on a train two years earlier. Back then, they had found an empty and forgotten structure in the middle of nowhere. Now it was full of new recruits, many of whom were younger than themselves.

"That's the fifth group in so many months," Tricia agreed, stirring her soup with her spoon. She didn't like to eat hot things and would wait until the concoction was at room temperature before eating it; just one of her many quirks that they'd grown used to in these last few years.

She spoke softly, leaning forward with her elbow on the table and visibly uncomfortable. She didn't like crowds of people, Jayson knew, and would have taken her meal elsewhere if it wasn't for the fact that she was trying to spend more time with Richard.

For his part, Richard usually ate meals with his wife outside the mess hall where they could be alone, but he was a social animal who loved to be surrounded by people. Still, Jayson doubted Richard even understood the sacrifice she was making for him.

"Hard to believe. Most of these recruits only arrived sometime in the last year and are already getting sent out on missions," Richard added. "Where do you think they are going?"

"Hard to tell," Jayson said. "They don't really fill us in on details like that."

Richard had a tray loaded with beans, bread, and some sort of runny meat paste that didn't look very appetizing. Jayson, like Tricia, had elected to try the soup, not willing to give the mystery meat a chance. The soup was bland and syrupy, but at least it was a known quantity.

Richard ate his meat paste with gusto, but Jayson had learned long ago not to trust Richard's taste when it came to food.

"We've been here longer than anyone else," Jayson added, a touch of bitterness creeping into his tone. "And by *many* months. Yet we're still here and everyone else is getting sent out on assignment."

"At least they let you try out the awesome armor," Richard said.

"I got shot in the chest."

Richard shrugged. "Still better than nothing."

"It still hurts."

"Maybe they have something important in mind for us," Tricia said, ignoring them. "They could be saving us for something."

Jayson shrugged. "Or maybe they just forgot about us."

"It's getting boring," Richard agreed. "I'm sick of just sitting here and going through training exercises. I'm ready to head out and actually *do* something. I don't care if it is just something small. There's only so much time we can spend on Alderson practicing and training before we go completely stir crazy."

"Agreed," Jayson said. "There are only a few of us left from the original group, and it's almost as though they don't even care that we are here."

"Yup," Richard said.

They fell silent, eating their meals and listening to the conversations around them. Jayson looked at all of the new faces, many of which he didn't recognize.

Their training regimens varied as much as the assignments they were being sent on. Some of them were just soldiers being taught how to fight and kill. Some were being shown how to start insurrections and cause dissent. Others were trained to infiltrate various governments and wreak havoc from the inside or as assassins that were given high-value targets to eliminate.

They were given a specialized skillset and single task and then sent out into the world. Of those who had already gone on missions, many were captured or killed. Others returned and were sent out again. Yet, through it all, the original arrivals were left behind just watching it all take place.

Unlike the recruits that were being given very specialized training, the skills Tricia, Jayson, Richard, and Bret had received encompassed everything, from etiquette and survival on various planets to starting and leading militias to assassinating politicians and creating havoc or starting riots.

All skills that were being wasted.

The room gradually cleared out as the students went off to sessions or classes until they were the only ones left. Jayson had long since finished eating, leaving half of his tasteless soup behind.

"What are we learning about today?" Richard asked, leaning back and stretching. "Hacking and digital networking?"

"I don't think so," Tricia said. "Bret is getting specialized training with it, but I think we're done learning about technology."

"So, nothing then?"

Tricia shrugged. "Free rein to do what we want, I guess."

"Do you want to go spar?" Jayson asked Tricia. Since they didn't have any current classes they were required to participate in, they were allowed to sit in on any lessons they preferred. Alexander Robertson had given them a standing offer to learn anything and everything they could, explaining that they would need it later.

For Jayson, that meant sparring and fighting. He liked to test his skills against the best, and there was no one better at the Academy than Tricia.

"Sure," Tricia replied.

"Not me," Richard said. "I'm heading off to take a nap."

Jayson shrugged and started to stand up. Just then, the door to the cafeteria opened and Alexander Robertson walked into the room. He was wearing a white suit and carrying his maple wood cane, tapping it on the ground every few steps. It made a hollow echoing sound in the room, reminding him of their first time in the cafeteria.

He hoped this wasn't a repeat of that event.

In his free hand Alexander was carrying a bottle of some sort of alcohol. He walked across the empty cafeteria to their table, moving carefully and quietly. He sat down next to Jayson and rested his cane against the table.

One by one, he gathered up their cups, dumped their contents onto the floor, and filled each with the liquid. It looked thick and syrupy as it poured out. Even from a few feet away Jayson could tell that it smelled horrible, like rotten fish. He set the cups out in front of each of them.

"I understand your concerns," he said finally. "And I want you to know that things are almost ready."

"You were listening to us?" Richard asked.

"We're always listening."

Richard coughed. "That isn't creepy at all."

Alexander didn't even acknowledge his statement. He picked up his own glass.

"Everything our graduates have done up to this point has been with the intention of solving local problems in our Sector. We've accomplished very little, but we've only been testing the waters for things to come."

"Then why not include us?"

"I couldn't, on the orders of Maven Ophidian."

"Why?" Jayson asked, shaking his head. "Why would she want to hold us back?"

Alexander hesitated. "Above my pay grade. Let's just say that she has something specific in mind for the four of you."

"Four of us?"

"Bret as well. The original arrivals at the Academy, hand selected by Maven for this specific mission. Soon you will be traveling to Sector Two."

"For what?"

Alexander shook his head. "I don't know. As soon as I have any details, I will let you know. In any case, let us toast to finally having a mission for you to undertake."

They glanced awkwardly at each other and then held up their cups to toast. They weren't glass, so they made a thudding sound rather than a clink when they touched.

Jayson watched Alexander swallow a mouthful before sipping his own beverage. It tasted oily and burned like fire as soon as it went down his throat. He found himself sputtering and coughing with tears in his eyes.

The others didn't fare any better. Tricia coughed and spat the drink back out. Richard took a big swallow and then made a gagging sound, clutching at his throat.

Alexander chuckled and set his drink down. "Takes some getting used to."

"What the hell is that?" Richard asked, wiping his mouth and wincing. "Tastes like burnt plastic."

"A prized beverage from my planet called Calampor. Sells for thousands of credits a glass in the right places. I've been saving this bottle for a special occasion."

"Special occasion?" Tricia asked.

"You'll be on your real mission as soon as you finish one last task," Alexander replied.

"Task? What do you have in mind?" Jayson asked.

"Clearing out a research facility," Alexander said. "Though I can't tell you more."

"Clearing out?" Richard echoed. "What does that mean?"

"Just what it sounds like. Some...things have taken up residence there, and once you clear them out, you'll be on your way to Sector Two and the real mission will begin."

"That doesn't sound so bad," Jayson said. "When do we start?"

"Soon. A few weeks. I'm going to get you out of the Academy for a while so you can enjoy a short vacation before your undertaking."

"Why would we need to leave?"

"Questions won't do you any good," Alexander said. "There are certain details I'm not allowed to divulge. Suffice it to say, you have made some powerful enemies, and there is a cost to that. I'll move you away from the Academy, and when it is time to begin your mission, you will know. Think of this time like a well-earned vacation."

"So then why the special occasion drink if we aren't actually graduating? Shouldn't you have waited until we are back before breaking open the bottle?" Jayson asked.

"We're drinking it now," Alexander explained, "because I'm not sure if any of you will survive."

2

Jayson leaned back against the tree, rubbing the cramp out of his inner thigh. "Some vacation this is."

"I thought he was sending us to a beach," Richard said. "Or at least somewhere we could relax. Instead he sends us here."

"Two weeks," Jayson said. "We've been sitting here for two weeks waiting for something to happen, but no word at all."

Alexander Robertson had separated them and flown them out of the Academy, but they were surprised to find out they were being dumped a few hundred miles north of the Academy with only modest supplies. They were told to stay put and wait for further instructions.

"You look angry," Richard said, rubbing the stubble on his chin and watching Jayson.

He looked different now: He'd shaved daily while at the Academy, getting rid of all facial hair, but now that they were out in the middle of nowhere, he'd let his beard grow back in. It was the Richard he remembered, though he did need some grooming to make it look good.

They had a few knives they'd fashioned since getting dropped out here, but nothing sharp enough to shave with.

To be honest, Jayson could fully understand why Richard had grown his beard out to begin with. His face was too lean, and his cheeks too sallow without it. When he was clean shaven, he looked ten years older and quite a bit less healthy.

Jayson sighed and stretched his leg out. The cramp was still there, but it was starting to go away. He closed his eyes in relief and yawned.

"I look angry?"

"Or constipated. I can't tell which, but it's all over your face."

"I'm just tired," Jayson said. "But I guess frustrated fits, too. How long are we supposed to just sit out here and wait for something to happen?"

"Maybe this is the mission."

"Like a survival mission? If it's a survival mission, then it's kind of easy when you really get down to it."

Richard shrugged. "True."

"It's just frustrating having nothing to do."

"Have you eaten anything today? You sure are a grumpy-pants."

"Half ration."

"You need to eat more."

"Not hungry."

"That's not the point," Richard said. He reached into his pack and pulled out a small package. Some sort of corned beef energy bar was inside, along with a hard biscuit and dried fruit. "Eat. You need the calories."

"I only need a few hundred calories a day to survive. These ration packs have over six thousand calories in them."

Still, despite his protest, he grabbed a sliver of dried apple and popped it into his mouth.

"You need more when your body is high functioning."

"We haven't been high functioning in weeks," Jayson replied, reaching into the container for some more of the dry fruit. He grabbed a handful of raisins. "We've just been stuck here, waiting. What are we waiting for?"

"No clue. Wish I knew, but it's crazy boring."

Jayson popped the raisins into his mouth and chewed thoughtfully. The boredom was getting to him, he knew, and Richard was right: He did need to eat. He spent a few hours each day exercising, but there was little else to occupy them.

At first, it was sort of relaxing. After the last few years of intense exercise and training, it was nice getting a chance to just rest and recuperate. Wilderness survival had become one of the easiest jobs in the world for them after their training.

Now they were sore from sitting, full of expendable energy, and unable to sleep. Jayson wanted to run a few kilometers or lift some weights, but it was hard to do out here in the middle of nowhere. He could only work out so much each day before he needed to rest and the boredom set in again.

"Do you think he forgot about us?" Jayson asked.

Richard shook his head, munching on the biscuit. "No. I think he's just testing us. Testing our loyalty, and maybe our ability to follow instructions. Do you remember when we were tossed out here the first time?"

Jayson chuckled. "When Alexander beat the crap out of us and left us for dead?"

"Yep," Richard replied. "When I almost died and you and Trish had to drag me along to keep me alive."

"Good times."

"Feel like stealing a train again?"

"Not yet. Ask me again next week if things don't pick up."

"At least they are feeding us this time."

Jayson held up a piece of fruit that had turned gray. "If this stuff can be called food."

Richard glanced down at his biscuit. "You know what this needs? Honey. Slop a little bit of honey on top, and it would be pretty damn tasty."

Four times now they'd been dumped off in the middle of nowhere in different quadrants of the planet. Alderson was notorious for having deadly wildlife, and it forced them to learn how to defend themselves in hostile environments.

The worst trip was actually a city that had long since been abandoned when the Academy was vacated by the Republic. Broken-down buildings that were overgrown with vines and weeds and vast landscapes covered in concrete made scavenging for food much more difficult than out here in the wilds.

Usually they were left in groups of two or three with limited survival equipment. The expectation was that they would be able to survive on their own and find their way home. The first two times— not counting that first survival experience—they were warned of the adventure in advance and given preparatory training. They were taught things like how to find water in a desert or how to dig for bugs to gain protein.

The other two times they were given no warning at all. Alexander woke them up in the middle of the night and dumped them off without even a map to find their way home.

This time was different, way more relaxed. Survival had become old hat to them now. At least the four that were left. So far, of the original seven that showed up at the Academy two years ago, only four were still in training. The other three had died along the way. They'd been left in unmarked graves, unknown to history.

A terrible way to die.

"Do you regret it?" Jayson asked.

"Regret what?" Richard asked, folding the bag of foodstuffs and shoving it back into his pack. He settled back against his tree and stared off into the woods.

"All of this," Jayson replied. "The Academy. The training."

Richard was silent for a minute. "I don't really regret coming here, no. I miss a lot of things from before, you know, but not enough that I want them back. The things they've taught us...I thought I knew how to kill people before, but this is something else."

"Was it what you expected?"

"Oh hell no," Richard said with a laugh. "I was expecting a straightforward military school. That's what the Academy used to be when it still belonged to the Republic. But Maven is something else; she thinks sideways. I wasn't expecting to learn how best to poison people or build bombs."

Jayson nodded. "Me neither."

"What about you? Do you regret it?"

Jayson wasn't sure. Some days he did and missed his family. He wanted to go home and see them. There were moments when he actually thought about leaving the Academy and fleeing home.

But most of the time he enjoyed it. He found it exhilarating and engaging, and he'd learned more in these last two years than the rest of his life combined. The training was intense and varied, and the expectations were high.

"No," he answered. "I don't regret coming out here."

"Yeah, why would you? I mean, this is where they trained the Fists back when it was part of the Republic."

"Have you ever seen one?"

Richard laughed. "No way. I don't know anyone who has. Fists of the First Citizen? I'm pretty sure if you see one of those, it means you're about to die."

"I heard they were ten feet tall."

"At least," Richard said. "They all wear powered armor and carry five-hundred-pound guns. Each of them is an army unto himself."

"Do you think the rumors are true that they are genetically engineered?"

"Definitely. Perfected humans capable of wiping out entire planets. I think that's what the research facility is all about. This is where they designed the Fists."

"You're kidding."

"Think about it. It makes sense. They trained the Fists here originally, which means if they *were* modified, they would have needed somewhere close to do it."

"So you think Darius is after the research?"

"Absolutely. He wants to make his own super-human soldiers."

Jayson hesitated. "Seems farfetched."

"It's illegal, but if you think the super-rich aren't already doing it, then you're crazy. They make their kids smarter, or faster, or healthier all the time."

"But the idea of engineering a human from scratch just seems..."

Jayson wasn't sure how to finish. To him, it sounded ridiculous. The Ministry taught that God stood against genetic engineering in all of its forms, and the Ministry was aligned very close to the Republic and its leadership. The idea that there might be engineering happening that they didn't know about, or worse, that they sanctioned, was difficult for Jayson to buy into.

"You know about the Shields?" Richard asked.

Jayson nodded. "Yeah, his personal bodyguards."

"The stories I've heard, they are engineered as well. They can do things with their minds."

"I don't buy it," Jayson said. "They are soldiers. Well-trained, sure, but they aren't genetically modified or anything."

"How do you know?"

"They come from the Ministry," Jayson said. "Maybe the Republic is doing some shady stuff behind the Ministry's back, but the idea that the Ministry would be in on something like that...there's no way."

Richard shrugged. "Maybe you're right. Either way, from everything I've heard, the Shields are badass as hell."

"I *have* heard that," Jayson said. "Even back on Eldun, we were told legendary stories about them. I didn't know much about what the Republic was, but I knew about the Shields. Most of it was probably fiction to scare off would-be assassins of the First Citizen, but it still made for great stories."

"What would you do if you met one?"

80

"Probably crap myself," Jayson said with a laugh.

Richard chuckled. "Me too."

They sat in silence for a good twenty minutes, just listening to nature around them. It wasn't too cold this far north, but Jayson knew only a little farther and it would be freezing.

"Ever been to Sector Two?"

"Nope," Richard said. "You?"

Jayson shook his head. "Always wanted to go, but it's just too damn expensive."

"What do you think we'll be doing there?"

"Spying. Infiltrating the government and reporting back."

"Won't be easy."

"I know," Jayson said.

"Do you think they'll have us launch any attacks? Muck things up?"

"No. Too risky."

"You sure about that?"

Jayson shrugged. "How sure can I be? I guess we'll know more soon enough."

He stood up and stretched. His muscles were still cramping from sitting too long, and he needed to move around a little bit. "I'm going to go for a run. You interested?"

"Nah, I'm good," Richard said. "I'll hold down the fort."

Jayson nodded, finished stretching, and then took off for a run through the trees. It felt good and he ran for several kilometers, circling around their camp and blowing off some steam. He saw various signs of wildlife, but nothing threatening while he was out there.

By the time he got back, it was nearing nightfall. Richard was in the same spot, and Jayson wasn't even sure if he'd moved. He knew Richard was pining over Tricia; it was the longest he'd been away from her in months, and he was probably worrying over the fact that she was spending so much time with Bret.

Jayson knew Tricia wasn't even remotely interested in Bret as more than a friend and companion, but he also knew he couldn't convince Richard of that. He was the jealous type, prone to worrying over little things.

"Did I miss anything?" he asked.

"Nope."

He dried himself off and then cracked open one of their few remaining rations. He would check their traps in the morning and see if they'd caught anything, but for now he just wanted something simple to eat.

Richard built up a fire and they sat on opposite sides of it, listening to it crackle as night fell.

"Tomorrow," Richard said suddenly, breaking the silence.

"What about tomorrow?"

"Tomorrow is when we're going to get our orders and start moving again."

"How do you know?"

"Just a feeling," Richard said. "My gut tells me we're going to be heading out soon."

"I'm not one to trust your gut," Jayson said, eating a piece of bread, "but I do hope you're right."

Chapter 8
Sector 6 – Eldun
Vivian Drowel

1

The little ship touched down inside the hangar bay in Delphi with a gentle thud. Vivian wasn't the greatest pilot, but she knew enough about flying to do a half-decent job, and she was pleased she managed to land without breaking anything.

It didn't help that the ship she was flying was one she didn't have a lot of experience with. The *Cudgel* was her old vessel, one she'd spent much of her life with, but she'd given it up a few years earlier to get water purification supplies to the people of Mali.

So now she was flying a junker that Argus had sent her, the sort of vessel that wasn't worthy of getting a name. Except maybe *Junker*, she decided. Maybe she should rechristen it sometime in the near future.

She would have greatly preferred to have Jack take care of piloting, but she'd left him back on Jaril a few days earlier. It had taken her a little longer to make it out to Eldun than she wanted, but she was confident the delay wouldn't throw her timetable off too much.

Traq was sitting in the copilot's chair, watching everything she did with childlike curiosity. He was a really smart kid, picking most things up after only a few tries. She had explained to him how the flight controls worked, and with only a little bit a training, she was certain he would have no problem flying on his own.

But that was an agenda for another day. Right now she wanted to teach him how the world worked and show him how to survive in all conditions. The Ministry didn't know about him yet, nor the Union, but she doubted she could keep him hidden forever. When they were forced to flee and live on the run, she wanted to make sure he wouldn't be a burden.

"Ready to go?" she asked.

"Uh huh," Traq replied, unbuckling his safety belt and hopping down from the seat.

She followed him to the loading ramp and took a few moments to lower it down. It let them out into a huge hangar bay. It was massive, enough to hold a small city, and mostly unoccupied.

This was a military complex, and the city of Delphi was currently under military law. They had only just won a war against their neighboring city of Briden's Ward and the peace was tentative at best.

Soldiers were waiting for them at the bottom of the ramp, but she wasn't concerned. She'd already gotten clearance to land weeks earlier, and checking in was merely a formality. Argus had pulled some strings on behalf of the Ministry, and after a few well-placed donations, he'd turned her into a regional diplomat on behalf of the Republic. It gave her immunity on most planets and let her travel anywhere with impunity.

She was confident that even in a time of war, they would honor her immunity. After all, no one wanted to piss off the Republic.

In the center of the soldiers stood a well-dressed man with a short black beard and a lot of medals on his uniform. He looked to be important, at least in his own mind; probably a commander of some sort.

He gestured with his hand toward a series of offices on the other side of the hangar.

"Please, follow me this way for processing."

"I was told we were already cleared."

"You are," the man said. "This is merely a formality. Your delay in arrival will need to be noted in the system and cleared. I have confidence we can have you out of here in only a few minutes."

Vivian and Traq followed him to the rooms, and the rest of the soldiers fell into line around them. They all looked grim and hardened, the sort of soldiers who grew up around battle and strife and knew nothing else. They looked as though all of the joy had been stripped from their lives.

She was like them, she knew, having grown up in the Ministry and served as a Shield. Life had never been easy, and it had taken a toll on her, just like it had all of these people. The civilians would be no different, she knew: war took the joy out of everything.

They stepped into the offices and the general turned to face her once more. She saw from a name plate on his chest that his family name was 'Coley.' It didn't list a first name.

Another soldier stepped behind a terminal and began swiping and inputting data, registering their arrival and making notes for future use.

"No weapons will be allowed in the city," the general said.

"Of course."

"You will have our full protection while you are inside of Delphi, but as soon as you leave, you will be on your own. The outlying territories are dangerous."

"I understand."

"Are you certain you wish to be dropped off in the wilds? Things can get rather dangerous out there, and we don't have full control. Banditry is a problem."

She nodded. "Yes. I sent coordinates this morning. We will make our own way back to Delphi."

The general nodded at her. "Very well. I have a ground vehicle standing by and a driver to take you to your listed coordinates. I wish you well, and trust that we will be able to count on your support in future endeavors?"

She had no idea what endeavors he might be referring to, but assumed it was something he'd run across Argus before allowing her to land. Probably elections or something she didn't need to be a part of.

In any case, it didn't really concern her. "Absolutely."

He nodded at her, and again at Traq, and then headed off. She decided she didn't like him. He seemed entirely too patriotic for his own good.

At least he was short and punctual.

The rest of the soldiers followed him, except for one, who stayed behind with her. It was the one who had been inputting her information.

"Ma'am, if you will please follow me," he said, heading outside of the hangar bay.

She followed, holding Traq's hand, to a wheeled vehicle parked around the corner. It looked armored and old, with a lot of dents and bullet holes. She doubted they had anything else to work with.

"Do we need to grab some supplies?"

"Already handled, ma'am. Compliments of the general."

"Is General Coley in charge of the city?"

"Yes, ma'am," the soldier said, climbing into the vehicle and turning it on.

She and Traq climbed in as well, and they sped off down the road toward one of the exits.

"How long has General Coley been serving?"

"His entire life," the soldier replied. "He retired some years back to be with his family, but when Briden's Ward attacked us, he came back to lead."

"His family lives in the city?"

"Yes, ma'am, except for his son, who left years ago. He was supposed to join up and follow in his father's footsteps, but he left. Couldn't stomach the thought of war, I suppose. It had a deep impact on the general, and he's never really forgiven his son."

"You think his son is a coward?"

"I don't have an opinion on the matter, ma'am."

The soldier fell quiet, just driving. They passed broken-down buildings and exhausted people going about their lives. It looked like they'd been hit with mortars or bombs sometime in the past.

No one smiled or even acknowledged their passing. A tall fence with barbed wire at the top surrounded the city, making it look more like an enormous prison than a city. Guards patrolled and protected all of the gates and entrances.

It was raining, turning the ground muddy and casting everything in gray shadow, making the city feel desperate and worried. Vivian had been to places like this; she had seen the frail existence war leaves behind. Fear consumed everyone and everything.

It was having an effect on Traq. He watched people walk along the streets, bent over and broken by the weight of their lives. There

86

was a concerned look on his face, and he didn't seem to know how to react.

"Is this what the entire city is like?" he asked.

The guard glanced at him in the rearview mirror and frowned. "This is what the entire *planet* is like."

"Wow. That...why doesn't everyone just leave?"

"We don't all have that luxury," the man said, an edge of resentment in his voice. He didn't look at Vivian when he spoke, but she could tell what he thought of them: rich tourists who got their way in anything.

Luckily, Traq didn't notice his resentment. He kept staring out the window, watching the city fly past and turn into open country. The city was built alongside thick copses of woods and forested territory. It was a beautiful planet, but every once in a while, they saw signs of old battles and destruction.

Vivian thought to ask the driver if he could drive them past the evacuated city she'd searched out along the way, but she changed her mind. He didn't seem to think this was a productive use of his time, and she didn't want to push her luck with them and end up stranded away from the coordinates she'd picked.

They would be hiking back this way anyway, so she wasn't too worried about missing the demolished city on the way out. Traq would experience it in time.

The driver was silent the entire rest of the way, which was fine with Vivian. She didn't particularly want to converse with him.

They drove for several hours before finally stopping in a clearing. It was the middle of the night, and Traq had fallen asleep several hours earlier in the backseat.

"These are the coordinates," the man said. "Will you be requiring anything else?"

"No," she said.

The man nodded at her. Vivian helped Traq out of the vehicle, but he didn't even wake up. She set him gently on the ground and then started grabbing their gear.

The soldier helped unload the supplies the general had procured for them, climbed back into his vehicle, and drove off. He didn't look back.

Vivian watched him disappear, listening to the sounds of nature around them. They were in the middle of nowhere, about halfway between Briden's Ward and Delphi, and there was no sign of any other people being nearby.

She unrolled a blanket and laid it overtop Traq and then settled back and relaxed herself. Part of her motives for coming out here were exactly what she told Jack: she wanted to expose Traq to every facet of life, even the bad things, to make sure he was prepared for anything life threw at him.

But part of her desire for this was something else. She hoped it would be one of those bonding experiences her books told her about. Traq had a strong connection with Jack, and if she was going to send Jack away and train Traq on her own, she needed him to develop a similar bond with her.

The only problem was, she didn't know how.

The books said to do what she loved to do with children. She loved the wilderness and hiking, and she was excited that this would be a relaxing vacation for the both of them. She promised herself she would go easy on him and make him like her.

2

God, she had never really expected children to be so frail.

Traq tried hard. He really did. He did everything that she asked of him and always gave it his all, but he was never quite able to live up to her expectations. If one thing wasn't going wrong, it was something else.

The problem was, so many of the general day-to-day things she'd assumed Traq could do for himself, she found out Jack had been doing for him. It was even *worse* than she'd imagined. He couldn't really prepare himself breakfast or pack his bags or any of the other simple things she took for granted that he knew how to do.

She would need to have a talk with Jack when they got back about responsibilities because if Traq wasn't expected to take care of himself, then he never would.

She'd managed to fix a lot of those problems early on because Traq was a bright kid. She taught him how to pack his bags properly—not just shoving items in—and prepare a meal, and after the second day of hiking, he was doing it perfectly. They quickly fell into a comfortable routine.

She would take him out running in the morning before they had breakfast to limber up their bodies for the day of hiking. He wasn't able to jog very far yet, but that was fine. They could take breaks and relax whenever they needed to because they weren't in a hurry.

The entire hike was a little over a week long if they pushed themselves, but right now, they were just setting a leisurely pace and enjoying the outdoors. She was loving it, the purity of the air, the simplicity of life. Growing up, excursions like this had been a luxury, and it was one of the few pieces of her childhood she looked back on fondly.

Occasionally, though, she did wish she could push Traq just a little bit harder. He needed a lot of breaks for water or to rest his feet. He didn't really whine or complain, but she could tell by the looks on his face and his breathing that this was difficult on him.

At first, it had frustrated her, though over time she'd come to understand that it was her failing, and not his, that put them in the position of diminished expectations. The fact of the matter was that she simply did not understand what it was like being a child.

Her childhood had been horrible and filled with pain and despair at the Ministry, and she'd blocked most of it out. She didn't remember much before her fifteenth birthday when she was chosen to train as a Shield for the First Citizen.

That was the moment she thought of as the beginning of her life. It was the day she was told she would be allowed to leave the Ministry and achieve something better than just being a test subject. She was destined for greatness, unstoppable out in the real world.

That was before her injury.

Now she was just damaged goods.

Right now, they were on their third day of hiking and had stopped for a while to rest and take care of some other tasks. They hadn't made a lot of progress yet on the actual journey, and she'd decided they could take a day to rest and relax before continuing.

The General had overstocked their supplies by a good amount, and if they stretched them out, they could survive out here for three or four weeks. Jack would be frantic if they took that long, but she wasn't terribly worried about that right now.

The other reason for moving slow was to make sure they didn't accidentally stumble into danger. Eldun was technically a part of the Indeil Kingdom but only by loose affiliation. There were six warring factions on the planet, and regional animosity made it a dangerous and empty place to live.

The problem was that Eldun was always bordering on war, and when the various factions weren't warring, they were looting and fighting over the scraps they hadn't managed to destroy. Bandits were something she had to keep her eye out for and avoid.

She spent some of their time training Traq in fighting. Jack wasn't around, which meant she didn't have to worry about him berating her about teaching him how to protect himself. It was another one of those things he felt Traq was too young for. Jack just didn't understand that what Traq needed was discipline, not a friend.

"Keep your leg up," Vivian said, walking slowly around Traq.

He stood in front of her, arms out to the sides and his left knee up in the air. He was balancing on his right foot and had been for the last forty minutes. He was starting to wobble to and fro, which meant he wouldn't last much longer.

"I'm trying," he said.

"I know," she replied. "But you were letting your knee slip down. There's no sense in doing the exercise if you aren't going to do it right."

"My legs are tired."

"They should be," she said. "You're almost done."

She continued walking around him, checking his positioning to make sure he wasn't cutting any corners. That was what this lesson was really about. She needed to make sure he understood that there was a right way to do things, and a wrong way, and it was never acceptable to do it the wrong way just because he was tired.

The wrong way was how someone ended up dead.

"Time," Vivian said. "You can relax."

Traq almost fell to the ground he was so tired, and the look of relief on his face was almost comically exaggerated.

"Are you hungry?" she asked.

"I'm tired," he said.

"Okay," she said. "You can take a short nap, but then we're going to have to get moving. We have another twelve kilometers to hike today before we can stop for the night."

He staggered over to his bedroll, but didn't even manage to get it unrolled before falling asleep. It was early in the afternoon and she'd been working him since just before dawn. Vivian watched him sleep for a moment and then finished unrolling his bedroll. She tucked him inside of it and then set off to scout the surrounding area.

She would let him sleep for about an hour or so, but then they really did need to get moving. They could afford to be a few days late in reaching the city and contacting Jack, but any longer than that and he might start to worry and come looking for them.

Or worse, he might get Argus involved in trying to locate her.

Up to this point, she'd kept her contact with Argus Wade to a minimum, and things seemed to be safe and under control on his end. But if something happened and the Ministry came hunting for her, she wanted to make sure they wouldn't have any easy time of finding her.

Jack didn't know about that side of her life though, and telling him about the *Ordo Mens Rea* would put them all at risk. She couldn't take the chance of him making a mistake and jeopardizing everything. She hoped it never came to that, but she knew what the Ministry and the Republic were capable of and wasn't willing to take any chances.

She hiked through the woods, enjoying the seclusion and trying to clear her mind. They were only a few days away from the broken city she'd come here in search of, and she was wondering if maybe she should just skip it.

The problem was, it was an embodiment of devastation and death, and even though she felt Traq *should* experience it, she was having second thoughts and doubts about whether this was the right time. Maybe Jack was right and he was too young. She'd been wrong about how much strain he could handle, so maybe she was wrong about this too?

Maybe it was better to just leave Traq be and not expose him to the previous incarnation of Delphi. He was a bright kid, and he knew right from wrong, so maybe this gesture wasn't such a great idea.

They could just turn this into a woodland hike and forget about the war. After all, a huge part of why they were out here was a bonding experience. That would be the best outcome, when she really got down to it.

Maybe she was getting better at this parenting thing...

3

She hiked around for about half an hour before she found signs that someone else was in the area. Boot prints in the dirt, and fresh ones at that.

At first she thought it might be from a group of Bandits or civilians, but after only a little bit more searching in the surrounding forest, she found a lot more boot prints as well as the tracks of ground vehicles.

A lot of them.

She started to get a sick feeling in her stomach as she scanned over the tracks. A force had come through here in the last few days, and not a small band but rather hundreds of soldiers with a lot of supplies.

It meant one of two things: either this was a small group of soldiers patrolling the area, or—much more likely—this was an advance group leading a much larger force that would be trailing a few days behind.

Either way, it was not something she had planned for, and it changed everything.

She needed to get Traq moving and get them back to safety as soon as possible. If this was a sign that the wars were about to start back up between Briden's Ward and Delphi, then she needed to get off world before something bad happened.

No more lollygagging. They needed to hike faster and get off planet before they ran out of time. Her priority was to keep Traq safe and get back to the ship.

4

It only took her a few minutes of heading back to her camp to realize that she had even less time than she'd anticipated. She found more tracks in the area of small bands of soldiers moving around behind her. They had managed to cut her off from Traq, and she cursed herself for straying so far away from her young charge.

They were very well organized, scouting the area in a pattern. Her worse fears were realized, and she knew that this was definitely part of an army: these were likely the advance scouts of an assembled army which was marching its way toward Delphi.

She had papers that gave her immunity in the region, but that meant nothing in the face of an advance army. They wouldn't care about any deals she'd made with Delphi for protection. They might even assume that since she had landed in Delphi, she was a spy working for them.

She couldn't afford to have any conflicts with this army, which meant they would need to change course and make a beeline directly back to Delphi. They would need to get off of Eldun before the army from Briden's Ward showed up.

She rushed back to their little camp, intending to wake Traq up and get moving, but when she got there, she realized she was already too late to avoid the scouts: they had found Traq.

Three uniformed soldiers were in their camp, two men and a woman. They were all facing away from her and wearing heavy armor. Each of them carried a heavy rifle. Two were rifling through their supplies, and the third was kneeling down in front of an exhausted-looking Traq, grilling him for information.

Traq looked bewildered and confused, keeping his mouth closed and looking around for her. Vivian let out a sigh and shook her head, preparing herself mentally for what she had to do. She tapped into the part of her mind linked to her implant and strode into her campground.

The two guards searching through her gear quickly stood up and raised their rifles as she walked calmly toward them.

"Halt!" the woman called.

Vivian stopped moving about three meters away, folding her arms in front of her chest.

"This is my camp," she explained.

"This is territory belonging to the city of Briden's Ward. You aren't locals."

"No, we are not," Vivian said.

"Do you have any authorizations that allow you to be here?"

Vivian hesitated. She didn't think the immunity Wade had gotten her would do any good right now, and it might actually be worse to give up their names and identities than to keep them to herself.

"We do not."

"Then you are trespassing," the woman said. "We will need to bring you in."

"No. I'm afraid you won't be doing that."

The woman narrowed her eyes at Vivian. "We will arrest you if necessary. I trust that it won't be?"

Vivian took a steadying breath. "You're welcome to try."

She lashed out through her implant, mentally seizing the barrel of the woman's rifle and jerking it sideways. She aimed it at the soldier standing next to her.

It had the expected effect: shock from both the woman and her partner. The man stumbled back, eyes going wide, and Vivian rushed forward. She closed the distance to the soldiers in a heartbeat, scooping a rock up along the way.

She kicked the man in the stomach, hitting him right in the abdomen under the ribs. He doubled over, clutching his stomach, and she followed through by smashing the rock against his jaw.

He fell heavily to the ground, dropping his rifle. Vivian mentally felt the woman struggling to push the barrel of her rifle back toward Vivian. She released her grip on the gun and the woman overcompensated, swinging the barrel past Vivian in the other direction. She pulled the trigger, but too late, and her shot went wide.

Vivian waded in with a series of attacks, punching the woman twice in the jaw and once in the neck, blocking her airway. She grabbed the gun—this time with her hand—and yanked the woman forward and off balance.

The woman collapsed onto her knees and Vivian kicked her in the face, knocking her unconscious.

The first man was struggling back to his feet, shaking his head to clear it. He had a huge red mark on his face where she'd hit him and was bleeding. Vivian walked past, kicking him in the face and knocking him out as well.

The third guard was raising his rifle and turning to face her. She lashed out mentally, knocking his barrel straight up in the air. He fired, but the bullet went well above her head.

She ran forward, closing the distance. Traq was behind the man now, and he dove forward into the back of his knees, tackling him. The man stumbled, pulling the trigger again and firing off a spray of rounds into the air.

Vivian closed the distance and kneed the man in the face. He fell backward and she bashed him in the temple with the rock, knocking him unconscious. Traq scrambled free from the man's legs and looked up at her, confused and scared.

94

"Where did you go?" he asked.

"I stepped out for a minute," she said. "Pack your things. We need to leave."

"They have guns," Traq mumbled. "They tried to *shoot* you."

"I know," she said. "Which is why we need to get moving. Everyone in a five-kilometer radius knows we are here now."

Traq looked like he wanted to ask more questions, but he read the look on her face well enough to know it wasn't a good idea. Without another word, he packed his bags. It only took five minutes before they were moving again.

As they walked, Vivian had to wonder just how bad of a situation she had gotten them into.

Chapter 9
Sector 6 – Eldun
Vivian Drowel

1

She finally allowed them to stop for rest a few hours later. Traq was exhausted, and she'd pushed them at a heavy pace. She had a headache from using her implant and it was throbbing just behind her eyes, making them water.

Using the implant wasn't something she'd done for a while, and it was the kind of skill that faded and became more difficult over time. She remembered during her time as a Shield that she could manifest her abilities for hours before the headache set in.

She would need to remember to practice more.

She forced Traq to drink some water and eat an energy bar before he passed out, but she knew the hike was too much for him. She would need to give him a chance to recover soon for longer than a few hours. His body simply couldn't keep up with the strain.

But they didn't have a lot of options. The advancing army knew she was out here now. No doubt those scouts had woken up and given their reports about why they had discharged their weapons. If they considered Vivian to be even a remote threat, they would send more soldiers after her and Traq, and they would easily be able to catch up with them in any of their vehicles.

Maybe she should have killed the scouts to keep her and Traq safe, but that wasn't a line she was willing to cross, not while she was with Traq, at least.

She didn't want to leave Traq while he was sleeping again, but she had to get an idea of what they were facing. She searched around the nearby area for a high tree she could climb to get a better lay of the land.

She found one only half a kilometer away and scurried up it. She reached the top branches and looked out, trying to get a view of what they were facing.

She couldn't see much because of the foliage, but she could see a large amount of smoke rising in the distance from countless campfires.

There were hundreds of them, enough for thousands of soldiers.

Probably a good thing she hadn't killed the scouts. She had to hope that they underestimated her and wouldn't send much of a response after them.

In any case, it was a problem she would have to face when it happened. For now, she just had to make sure Traq was doing okay and keep moving. It would take several more days even at a fast pace to get to Delphi. She just had to make sure they got there ahead of the army.

2

"I'm so tired," Traq whined, staggering along next to her.

It wasn't the first time he'd said it, nor even the first time this hour, but to his credit, he was complaining a lot less than Vivian expected. They were well into the next day of hiking, and they hadn't managed to stop for a sizable break since they'd first spotted the army.

Traq plodded along beside her, eyes on the ground and unfocused. He was starting to falter in his movement, and she knew he wasn't going to keep going much longer. He was exhausted well beyond what he could handle.

Twice, though, she'd tried to stop for a longer break than a few minutes and heard the sound of approaching vehicles behind them. They were sticking to heavily wooded areas that the vehicles couldn't get into, and they took roundabout paths and avoided open areas so the scouts couldn't cut them off, but the rapid pace was starting to drain Traq.

"Won't be much longer," Vivian said. "We can stop just around that next bend."

"Really?" he asked, perking up and looking ahead.

"Yeah," she said.

She was carrying both of their packs now, knowing there was no way he would be able to keep moving while carrying his modest supplies.

She was feeling it herself, too. Her legs were weak and she was mentally and physically exhausted, but she needed to keep up a tough exterior for Traq's sake. If he thought she was struggling, then it would only be worse for him.

They kept walking, the only sound their breathing as they moved through the forested area. It had been several hours since they'd last seen any sign of the scouts, and she was getting hopeful that they'd lost them.

Vivian knew she would need to carry Traq soon if they weren't able to rest, but hopefully they would find somewhere to stop for the night before it came to that.

"Are those people still chasing us?" he asked as they walked.

"I don't think so," Vivian replied. "I think we might have gotten away."

"Why were they after us?"

"Because they are afraid we will warn Delphi that they are coming."

He paused. "Will we?"

"I don't think it will come to that."

"Will they keep searching for us?"

"I hope not," she replied.

She doubted the scouts had even reported the incident as a real threat. Considering it was a lone woman and child that had handled them so efficiently, they would probably just drop it and pretend it never happened. Admitting what had actually happened—that they were beat up by an unarmed woman and child—would make them a mockery in their camp with the other soldiers.

"You said it was just up ahead," Traq said after another hour of walking.

"It is," she said. "Just around that next bend."

"That's a *different* bend," he argued.

"Well, then this is the one," she said. "We're almost there, I promise."

They got a lucky break about twenty minutes later when she spotted some ruins up ahead. With the blistering pace they been making for the last day, it looked like they'd found the abandoned city after all. She didn't have time to worry about whether or not Traq shouldn't see something like this now. She was just hoping they might find shelter.

Funny how the threat of death took away such trivial concerns.

She was certain they would find somewhere to lie low in there. With any luck, they could at least rest for a couple of hours before they had to move again. Enough time to catch their breath and take in a good meal.

They kept moving, and it took about another half hour of walking to actually reach the city. This was where Delphi used to be located, she knew, but after the last war, the cost of rebuilding the city had been too great and they had elected to move it. Now, it was just abandoned and neglected.

It was bigger than she'd expected, stretching into the distance with the skeletons of buildings and toppled structures lying on the ground. It looked like skyscrapers had been torn down in explosions, leaving nothing but devastation in their wake.

"We'll find somewhere in here to rest for the night," she explained.

Traq nodded but was too tired to respond by this point. He was panting and his legs were shaking, but he wasn't complaining. He was barely able to keep moving, and she was impressed with his tenacity.

They moved through the city streets and the structures, shifting around the rubble and wreckage. The city had been destroyed and abandoned twenty years ago, forgotten by the people who once lived here.

Eldun was an interesting planet because they had dangerous modern weaponry purchased from planets like Jaril, yet their politics and attitudes reflected more primitive societies engaged in isolationist politics and warfare that was all but eliminated from larger worlds.

Those advanced weapons they acquired could cause considerably more damage than they would have been able to if they had been left to their own devices.

In the Republic, a planet like Eldun would have been forbidden from purchasing or using weapons like this. The heavy hand of the First Citizen would have forced peace on Eldun years ago. It might not have solved the root problems, but it would have saved many lives.

Sure, the Republic had its own problems, especially where the Ministry was concerned, but at least they wouldn't allow a planet to simply murder poor civilians the way planets in the Indeil kingdom could.

"Here we go," she said, steering Traq toward a relatively intact structure a decent ways off of the main roads. It looked to have once been an underground facility for ground vehicles, though much of it had collapsed in the preceding years.

Somewhere deeper in the structure, she heard the dripping sound of water, but she didn't think exploring would be a good idea. It looked stable enough to offer shelter around the edges, but not sturdy enough to trust near the interior. Plus, they had plenty of water in their supplies for a few more days.

Traq collapsed to the ground just inside, leaning against a wall and taking deep breaths. He closed his eyes and laid his head back against the cement.

"I'm dizzy."

"It'll pass. How do you feel?"

"I hurt."

"That's good. It means your body is trying to heal itself back up," she said. "We'll rest here for a while, so get some sleep."

Vivian sat near the entrance, keeping one eye on her young charge and the other on the street outside.

She doubted the army would come through here. It would be difficult to get jeeps or vehicles over the rough terrain, and it wouldn't cost them a lot of time to simply pass around the city. She figured they were still a ways ahead of the army, maybe a day or two, but that meant the scouts wouldn't be far behind.

The sun slipped down below the horizon, making it difficult to see very far in any direction. There were no lights this far away from Delphi, and on a cloudy night like this, it turned pitch black. She closed her eyes, focusing on the sounds of the night and listening for any approaching footsteps.

3

Vivian was more exhausted than she'd realized because at some point she started dozing off. Her head dipped down to her chest, and she fell asleep.

She felt a tapping on her shoulder and reached up sharply, grabbing the finger touching her. Her other hand slid to the gun at her hip and began drawing it out.

She relaxed when she realized it was Traq.

"What? What is it?"

He winced and held a finger to his lips, then he pointed toward the exit of the parking structure. It took a second and then she heard the scuffing sound of a boot. It was a long way off, barely noticeable, but now that she was listening for it, she could hear a group of approaching soldiers somewhere outside in the abandoned streets.

Traq had a frightened expression on his face. She reached out and gently squeezed his shoulder, nodding at him to let him know things would be okay, and then slowly climbed to her feet. Her body was exhausted and stiff, but she was used to the feeling and knew how to force herself past the strain.

This was the sort of conditions she had been trained to fight in as a young girl. She was taught to battle and kill, especially when her body was weak and broken and she felt helpless. Her teachers would beat her and push her past the breaking point and still expect her to fight back.

This was what her mentors had prepared her for, and as the danger intensified, the adrenaline brought her back to those experiences as a little girl.

She tested her implant and drew in a steadying breath. Her first headache hadn't gone away from using the implant a few days earlier, but it wasn't enough to hinder her. She crouched near the entrance to their little hiding place and waited, listening.

No doubt whoever was approaching would have night vision technology—something she hadn't thought would be necessary in this little excursion—which gave them an upper hand. She would need to hit them hard and fast.

She listened and estimated that there were four soldiers at least. A difficult, but not insurmountable, group.

She reached into her backpack as quietly as she could and removed a flare. There was a chance their night vision goggles would protect them against sudden bright flashes with flare compensation, but that was a risk she would need to take. In either case, she wouldn't be able to take them on in the dark, and she could at least even the playing field.

The footsteps drew closer and she held her breath, waiting for them to either notice her and Traq inside the structure or move past. She felt the hairs standing up on her neck, and her muscles clenched, ready to spring into motion.

A long few seconds passed and then the footsteps passed beyond the building. They hadn't bothered to check inside and had no idea that anyone was hiding out. Vivian waited until they were a decent ways off before allowing herself to breathe once more. She turned to Traq.

"Stay here," she whispered. "Out of sight."

Then she slipped out of the structure and onto the street. Her eyes had adjusted fairly well to the night, and she could see enough to spot the moving shapes up ahead. She crept along behind them, finally catching up with the soldiers after a few minutes.

She stayed behind rubble and debris and trailed them. There were five of them, but she couldn't tell if it was that same first group of scouts plus a few more or an entirely different team. They weren't very attentive, never giving any structure more than a cursory glance, but they were armed and armored in fairly extensive gear.

She followed them for another ten minutes until they made their way out of the city and disappeared back into the woods. She was surprised, though, that they headed toward Delphi instead of back toward the army from Briden's Ward. These weren't advance scouts for the army but rather scouts for Delphi.

Which meant they must know about the approaching army. She had been hoping to make it back inside the city before they upped their defenses, but it looked like that was going to be more difficult now.

She had more pressing matters to worry about just now, though. That meant the scouts from Briden's Ward were still out there. She headed back and found Traq in the shelter. He was huddled up and waiting for her.

"Are they gone?" he asked after a minute, chewing.

"Yes," she said. "They left. We're really close to Delphi now, so we should be there by tomorrow or the next day at the latest."

"Okay," he said.

She took some food out of her pack, and she started eating: peanut protein bars that were slimy and tasted stale. It looked like the General hadn't stocked her the freshest of rations.

"We need to eat," she said. "Keep up our strength. Here."

She handed him another of the protein bars.

"I hate those."

"You need to eat."

He sighed and accepted the offered bar, taking a small bite of it the way a bird might. Then he scrunched up his face in exaggeration and made gagging noises.

She ignored him, knowing he was only doing it to get a response.

"Good thing you heard them," she said instead.

He shook his head. "I didn't hear them."

"Then how did you know they were out there?"

He shrugged. "I woke up, and I had a feeling. It was…I just knew they were out there."

She hesitated. "Just knew?"

"Yeah," he said. "It's like I could *feel* them."

She chewed quietly on her food, trying to decide what that meant. She knew a lot of people from the *Ordo Mens Rea* who could sense others like Traq was describing from her years spent at the Ministry and with the Shields. Wade had been able to do it a little bit, and some of the other Shields had been considerably more adept at it.

She'd never been able to do anything like that. Her powers stemmed more toward telekinesis and fighting. So did Traq's, she had assumed, since she saw him throw a kid through the air a few years earlier.

The thing was, very few members of the *Ordo Mens Rea* could handle *one* ability effectively, let alone multiple, and the idea that Traq could manifest two completely different powers without an implant was unthinkable.

But maybe not for Traq, she decided. He hadn't ceased to amaze her yet, so why should this be any different?

"Get some sleep," she said. "As soon as it's light enough, we're going to keep moving."

Chapter 10
Sector 6 – Jaril
Oliver Atchison

1

Oliver was bored.

It wasn't that he disliked the party at the Cortet family estate. The women were beautiful in their flowing, multicolored dresses and the men were dignified in well-cut business suits. The conversation was pleasant and mild with a lot of fake smiling and giggles.

The music was traditional and light and carried by excellent acoustics and speakers. The banquet was both simple and elegant. Free-floating chandeliers bathed the guests in a soft glow. This was old money, Oliver knew. The kind of money that shamed his dreams and aspirations.

There was nothing wrong with the decorations in the great dancing hall to make him so bored. It was just that all of the people were vapid simpletons. In fact, the most depressing part of the entire evening was the distinct *lack* of adversity.

He was accustomed to being invited to such gatherings and listening to people prattle on about how undeserving he and Jim were of their accolades and new station. That had been the norm for the past two years since they had been raised up.

And it made sense: Jim Crater was not a blood member of the Royal Family, so technically could not hold the position he'd been granted. They had adopted him, an archaic practice of adopting adults that hadn't been used in hundreds of years, but it was never going to be enough for the other wealthy and important people to accept them.

For the lay people, Jim was like something out of a storybook. A civilian hero that had risen up to protect his people. It was all ridiculous, but the idea had caught ahold of the public imagination.

But, for the actual royalty, Jim and Oliver were an affront to their dignity, and they loved to discuss their displeasure through gritted teeth.

Oliver was used to taking the jibes in stride. He accepted each offense with one crafted pleasantry or another. Usually, after suffering through a few hours of offensive idiots, he would be left to his own devices at the party to eat their food and drink their wine.

That was also when his window of opportunity opened up in his side dealings. Forgotten and ignored, he was able to move about the party as Oliver the Underworld Trader rather than Oliver the Ungrateful Hero. Some members of the upper echelon were ignorant and biased, but many more were willing to work with Oliver...at least when profit was involved.

Oliver didn't mind traversing the seedier parts of the city Mys. He grew up on these streets and knew them inside out. He acted as a middleman for the nobles, helping grease palms and make back-alley deals. In the last two years, he had made enormous profits and culled many favors from important people.

And many of those important people were here tonight and interested in trying to make deals. But frankly, Oliver wasn't in the mood to talk to any of them.

He was looking for one woman in particular.

2

The estate of Margaret Cortet was enormous; she was a first cousin to the king, but she was not known for her political aspirations. The estate encompassed thirty-six separate guest and servant housings and boasted a staff of over two hundred butlers and maids.

The manor was some forty thousand square meters with seven separate wings. It was surrounded by kilometers of carefully tended gardens, streams, and walking paths.

The Cortet family had built a reputation for avoiding the public spotlight. With socialized media and modern technology, it was difficult to remain anonymous, but the Cortet family fought long and hard for their obscurity. This was the first time Oliver had heard of them hosting *any* sort of gathering, and he didn't recall seeing them at any other nobleman's house in the last two years either.

Lady Margaret, it turned out, wasn't a child. She had grown into a woman in her late twenties with flowing green hair. She had pleasant features when she smiled and carried herself with an air of authority.

She had undergone a new skin treatment, tinting her skin a faint blue. It was exotic and enticing and popular with the nobility, but he wouldn't have called it attractive. Some people tried a little too hard to stand out.

There was a clutch of women following after her, murmuring and giggling to each other. She swept about the hall offering pleasantries and introductions, never staying in one place for too long. She was the perfect hostess, always in control.

When she finally made her way to Oliver, she expressed her deepest regrets that Admiral Crater hadn't been able to come, but hoped that Oliver felt as welcome as a member of her family. The surprising thing was that, when she said it, she had seemed genuinely upset that Jim hadn't shown.

Then she had disappeared just as fast, heading back into the crowd to greet the next visitor. All of the other guests, men and women who usually mocked him, were generous and polite to Oliver, always keeping one eye on the hostess as though they were children expecting to get chided. They were taking their cue from the hostess and treating him with civility.

The false pleasantness of it all was wearing him out more than the insults.

Somehow, the beautiful brunette he had come to see managed to sneak up on him.

He felt a hand brush his shoulder and turned to see the most elegant woman in the world smiling at him. Elizabeth had shoulder-length wavy hair and a shimmering silk gown that accentuated her curves perfectly. Yet it was her eyes that always caught Oliver's attention: deep amber, piercing and intelligent. He felt like he could fall into those eyes and drown. They were the real reason he'd come to Lady Margaret's banquet, just on the off chance he might get to peer into them.

Oliver had rarely seen Elizabeth with her hair down. Normally it was drawn back into a braid, and he'd certainly never dreamt of seeing her in such an expensive gown. He'd never seen her at such an elaborate gathering before, choosing only to meet with her on the streets when they had business to attend to...or other things.

It wouldn't do to be caught in a tryst with the sister of Admiral Hektor Mensch.

3

Oliver had fallen in love with Elizabeth Mensch months ago. He thought of himself as always in control of his emotions...always honest about his feelings. That was before he'd met Elizabeth.

"Care to dance?" she asked.

Don't grin like an idiot, Oliver told himself.

"Of course," he said, grinning like an idiot.

He took her hand and gently led her away from the tables. The dance floor was a practical location to have a private conversation: With sound dampeners, it would be impossible for their words to be overheard. But Oliver had to admit that whether or not it was a practical decision never really crossed his mind.

"How are you, Liz?" he asked, breathless.

"Well enough."

"I wasn't expecting to see you here."

"Neither was I. I'm surprised she invited you. Lady Margaret is one of my dearest friends."

He saw the corner of her lip twitch. "You don't know her at all, do you?"

"Why would you think that?"

"You have a tell. Be honest, you've never met her before today, have you?"

"No," Elizabeth admitted. "Not before this gathering. But I like her a lot. She's not as pretentious as I expected and more ambitious than I gave her credit for."

"How is your brother?"

She winced, a hurt expression in her eyes. He worried that someone might notice, but a quick glance around showed him that they were alone. There were another six couples on the dance floor, but with the size of the hall, there could have been upward of sixty couples without anyone coming close to them.

"I'm not here because he sent me," Elizabeth said. Oliver met her eyes. She looked down, the embodiment of false modesty. "Well, not entirely."

"He still gives you orders?"

"He's in charge of the family."

"You should be in charge."

"I will be," she replied. "But, for now, I have to play by his rules."

Oliver shrugged. "I'm not much for playing by the rules myself."

"I know," she said, smiling. She twirled, keeping in step with the music, and came close again. "I am *supposed* to be watching out to make sure Lady Margaret never speaks with your friend."

"Who, Jim? You thought he'd be here?" Oliver asked. "When has he ever come to a party?"

"Well, my brother thought that with the proposed engagement, he couldn't refuse—"

Oliver stumbled. "Hang on, hang on, what?"

Elizabeth scrunched her face up and then burst out laughing. "He didn't know, did he?"

"The countess wants to *marry* him?" Oliver said, possibilities whirling around his head. "Marry *him?*"

"A marriage of convenience," Elizabeth explained. "Her father is quite ill, and she has no desire to marry anyone who would absorb her legacy. Jim Crater is the lowest partner she can stoop to without reaching into the rabble."

"Yet no one told us?"

"That's what the invitation was for," Elizabeth said. "Business like this is never discussed with indiscretion. Margaret would only do it in person."

"He never comes to things like this."

She shrugged. "In any case, I believe the countess intended to solidify the arrangement tonight, and I was instructed to ensure the two of them never met."

"Would you have?"

"I was instructed to," she replied, pursing her lips. "But it is a *big* room. I doubt I would have been able to stop her from speaking with Jim."

"There is no love lost between you and your brother, is there?"

"He's a petty tyrant," she replied. "And he used to be a spoiled baby. Why should I care what he wants? I only took this job because I was afraid if Hektor gave it to anyone else, they might actually succeed."

"Should I call Jim? Tell him to get his butt over here?"

"That is up to you," she replied.

He hesitated and then shrugged. "It isn't really my problem."

"No, it isn't."

"Plus, I can think of some better ways to spend our time."

He stepped in close and kissed her. Her eyes went wide, but she didn't shy away. Finally, she pushed him back.

When they separated, she spoke breathlessly. "Trying to get us killed?"

"It would be worth it."

"Not when it's so easy to *not* get caught. People don't care what happens behind closed doors as long as you don't flaunt it."

"You know, I had an uncle that said the *exact* same thing right before marrying his goat."

"No you didn't," she said, chuckling.

"What? How would you know? Don't tell me you've looked into *my* past," he asked, pretending to be surprised. "Have you checked into my background?"

"Only the bad parts."

"It was a prize goat," Oliver explained, then before she could stop him, he leaned forward for another kiss. This time, she was slower in pushing him back.

"We should go," she said.

Her smell was intoxicating. "I agree. But there are a lot of people around that would see us leave together."

"True," she said. "In any case, I'm leaving."

"Where should I meet you?"

"That's for you to figure out," she said.

She stepped back, flashed him a smile, and then walked over to Lady Margaret. They spoke for a few moments and then Elizabeth headed for the exit. A moment later, he saw two men disappear from the crowd after her. Doubtless her brother's spies, keeping track of her whereabouts.

Oliver watched her disappear and sighed.

One day she's going to get me killed, he told himself. No woman is worth that kind of trouble.

It was understandable that Hektor Menschen wouldn't want a union between Crater and Lady Margaret to come to fruition. If Jim married into the family, then any chance they had of ousting him was gone forever.

It would also be a good move for Lady Margaret. Jim was an Admiral, even if it was only in name. It would help her standing and garner her some public sympathy if she did plan to leave the shadows and take on a more public role.

Truly, though, Oliver wasn't sure the marriage was a good idea. Lady Margaret wanted the matrimony as a political weapon. Leverage she could use against her enemies. She would probably rely on the fact that Crater was so much lower born than her to keep him in check.

She didn't know how infuriating he could be, and making Lady Margaret angry would be an unfortunate circumstance for both of them. Such a marriage was the perfect plan to solidify Jim's position as Admiral, if only he wouldn't screw it up. But screwing it up was inevitable.

Still...

Maybe he *should* call Jim and tell him about it. It wouldn't be fair to withhold that kind of information when it could solve all of Jim's problems.

In fact, the more he thought about it, the better the possibility seemed. If it worked out, and Jim didn't mess everything up, then there was a lot of profit to be had. 'First Officer' had a nice ring to it, and Oliver wondered what it would be like to be in such an important position.

Oliver reached into his pocket for his communicator. His fingers brushed against his jacket pocket, and he felt a bulge from something that he hadn't put in there. Curious, he reached in and found a little square key tag.

He eyed it for a moment, spotting the engraved name, and realized it was a hotel key. It belonged to a room in one of the most expensive suites only a few blocks from here.

Elizabeth must have slipped it in there while they were dancing.

Suddenly all thoughts of political intrigue flew out the window. He glanced back at the party one last time, trying—and failing—to convince himself he should stay, and then headed out the door.

Jim could solve his own problems.

Chapter 11
Sector 6 – Jaril
Jim Crater

1

When Crater arrived at the noblewoman's manor, his mood soured even further. The frivolity of the Cortet family was disgusting; they wasted money on useless things. Get rid of a few fountains and he could mount a gun on the *Cudgel*. Not that he needed a gun, but it would serve better than fountains.

Scale the central manor down to half the size and he could buy another ship. Hell, a *fleet* of ships. He hated having to come and beg on knee for favors from people whose only success in life was popping out of the correct womb.

Why would he even *want* to be a noble? The more he thought about it, the more he realized just how pathetic these people were. They had adopted him into the Royal Family and were reneging on their promise. He didn't want to be one of them. He still had his dignity.

Unfortunately, right now it had a low return on investment.

Worse, the guards at the cathedral door gave him a disgusted look as he limped toward them. He cursed his bad foot and the woman that gave it to him. But he doubted that alone was why he earned their scorn. To be fair, he wasn't wearing clothes fitting for such a pretentious gathering, but he was still a recognized dignitary, damn it. They had no right to question him.

A look of recognition dawned on one man's face as Jim drew near. "Sir," the guard on the left said, snapping to attention and saluting. The other spared only a sideways glance before mimicking his compatriot. "Lady Margaret is expecting you."

"What?" Jim asked, confused. Expecting him?

"Enjoy the party, sir," the guard said, opening one door as his partner opened the other.

Crater nodded and walked past. Their quick respectful response did much to lift his flagging spirits. He entered the gloomy interior of the great hall. It was a big room, annoyingly so, and stupid pictures decorated the walls. A butler greeted him and began guiding him farther into the chamber.

There weren't a lot of guests. Either the party was winding down or Margaret wasn't very popular. He didn't spot Oliver, but he did see a large group of women to one side of the hall. One woman stuck out in the group, wearing a more expensive gown. She looked to be in her early twenties. *Isn't Margaret young?* Jim thought Oliver told him she was only a child, twelve or thirteen.

The woman was standing near a buffet table. It was covered in a sampling of what appeared to be the most exotic foods the caterers could round up: little balls of some kind of fish, a bowl of syrupy fruit, and some sort of cheese wrapped in green leaves. Most of it looked inedible.

Crater was used to eating dry rations. He decided to steer clear of the odd fish substances and vegetables.

His eyes wandered and spotted an open bar.

He refused to acknowledge it. He focused back on the young woman. She was beautiful. She lacked the frumpy face and dark skin of the current King and his Wife. *It has to be her. Lady Margaret.* She spotted him across the hall and headed his way, her entourage falling in like a flock of well-dressed ducklings.

Margaret was in a red dress that shimmered and perfectly contrasted her flowing green hair. Her skin showed a blue glossy treatment that some prominent women were indulging in. It was a current fad, and when Crater had heard about it on the intranet, it sickened and annoyed him.

Any skin treatment costing the same as a new air filtration system was a total waste. But hearing about it and seeing the actual

114

effect had no comparison. It gave Margaret an exotic appeal that made him wonder just what it would feel like to touch.

Not that I'd ever get the chance to find out. Oliver maybe, but not me. It's probably toxic anyway. She bowed her head as she came to him. He bowed low in return, sweeping his Safari hat before him.

"Admiral Crater," Margaret said, smiling and gently touching his arm. "I'm so pleased you could make it."

"I am as well, my Lady," he said, taking her right hand and brushing his lips against her rings and finger. *Hopefully not toxic.* "I had some urgent business to take care of in the city. I pray you will forgive my tardiness."

"Of course. Unfortunately, I believe that the party is winding down. I am soon to retire."

Crater nodded, resigned. "I understand. I'm sorry that I couldn't come earlier." *For the best, I suppose.* "Pray, do you know where my friend is? Oliver."

She smiled a knowing smile. "He left earlier."

There's more you aren't saying, he knew, but he didn't press the issue.

"I was wondering if you would like to join me for a light supper," she said, drawing him from his thoughts. "It is already prepared."

Jim was caught off guard. "I...uh...absolutely," he stammered. Margaret nodded, slipped her arm through his. She nodded to her delegation to signal that they would be moving.

As soon as they were outside the hall, she began to chatter, leaving him no room to talk as she discussed a wide range of topics from seasonal weather to modern music and art. Jim barely heard her, wondering what had inspired this odd circumstance.

They passed a fountain with an angelic being spraying water out of a harp.

She led him through a garden decorated with exotic and colorful flowers, well tended.

What could she possibly want from me? She was noble, a blood cousin to the King, and doubtless among the group of people who had the most to lose by Jim's rise to fame. *So why is she being so friendly?*

But there was a simple explanation: She is going to make me work for her. Doing something illegal, most likely. And when someone in the Royal Family demands something, I cannot refuse. Great, just great. I shouldn't have come after all, Crater thought. The prospect of fleeing from Jaril seemed much more difficult with a noblewoman breathing down his neck.

She prattled on until they came to a veranda. It sat beside a beautiful pond just inside the eastern walls of the estate. She sat down, and her retinue fanned out around the veranda, taking up pre-designated positions. Jim realized some of them were well-trained guards pretending to be guests. The thought made him respect Margaret more. This might all be a game, but at least she seemed to know how to play it.

They sat in silence as servants brought food to the table. Crater was starving, and everything smelled delicious. He hadn't eaten since the day before and his stomach rumbled. He finished a bowl of a thin soup of mushrooms and leeks and then moved onto the second dish. It consisted of a choice cut steak—rare—and smothered in an orange-flavored peppery gravy.

There were also some of the rarest fruits, vegetables, and starches from a dozen planets, prepared in a variety of different ways. He helped himself to two bowls of a thick gray soup with chunks of brown cheese floating in it.

Jim moved swiftly from one dish to another. *Delicious,* he thought. *I hadn't realized I was so hungry.*

A dawning realization crept into his mind: These were all of his favorite dishes. He stopped eating suddenly and looked up to see Margaret smiling at him. She had barely touched the food.

"Are you enjoying the meal?" she asked.

"Yes," he said. *I get the feeling I'm supposed to.* He hoped she hadn't been planning to poison him; he had no governor where food was concerned.

"I am quite pleased that you made it to my home today. I was worried that you might not arrive."

Jim hadn't brought a weapon. He was regretting it.

"I had some business to attend to," Jim said, and something in her eyes told him she knew *exactly* what sort of business. He fought the urge to shift in his chair. He was an admiral, not a child scorned by his mother. He had nothing to be ashamed of.

"I see," she said, then, "there was something I wished to discuss with you. A mutually beneficial offer of support. My father had a modest fleet of ships built up over a number of years. He prayed for a son who might one day join the Admiralty, but alas I was an only child. All thirty ships are mine now, but I have no purpose for them. I would like to give them to you."

Jim stared at her. Was she taunting him? *What game is this?* No one just offered a fleet of ships.

A waiter came up onto the veranda, handing them cups of a sweet-smelling black tea.

A robed man raked gravel in a pit nearby.

The servant bowed and left. Jim took a sip. It was flavored with honey and tasted faintly of Jasmine. Once again, one of his favorites, and he was more than a little annoyed. He didn't enjoy being manipulated.

"No one just *gives* ships away. So you want something in return," he suggested. He took another sip of the tea, cursing himself. Why did it have to be so delicious? But he was determined not to give in to her agenda. Not without a fight at least.

No one uses Jim Crater.

And yet...

If Margaret *was* willing to sell him her father's fleet, he might be able to convince the Royal Family to extend his position. At least for a few more years. And with a fleet, he could recruit and make a name for himself. He might even be able to—

"On the contrary, it *would* be a gift," Margaret countered, sipping her own tea. "A wedding gift."

Jim dropped the tea cup. It hit his lap, spilling tea all over him, and crashed into the ground. He barely noticed. A servant was already on the way with a small broom and pan to sweep up the broken dish, but Jim waved the man away. "A what?"

"A bride's gift, specifically," she repeated. "A dowry, to use old custom. My father has been getting sick, and he has been pressuring me to wed before he dies, so I've been searching around for a possible husband that—"

"Wait, wait," Jim said, grabbing a towel off the table and wiping the tea off his lap. It had almost no effect. "Married...to me?"

She smiled weakly. "Yes, of course. Does that thought displease you?"

Jim found himself shaking his head as though in a daze. "No," he muttered. *Marriage? She's noble, and I'm...*

"Yes, of course I accept."

It didn't exactly require a lot of thought.

The next half hour flashed past. Servants brought documents out for them to sign as well as pastries to nibble. He agreed to everything Margaret said or asked and signed all the papers she brought forth. It felt like he was in a dream; none of it seemed real. Even if she had tried to slip something past him—which, he discovered later when Oliver went over the documents, she didn't—he was still making out like a bandit simply by acquiring her name. The fleet was icing on the cake.

But if it isn't me she's trying to screw over, then who is it?

When he finally stumbled back to the *Cudgel*, he found he was elated. The entire walk from the Cortet Estate had taken over an hour, but he barely remembered it. Oliver was already there, smoking his pipe and grinning in the cockpit with his feet propped up. *Maybe he already knows,* Jim wondered, though he doubted it. Oliver must have been happy about something else.

"What is it?" Oliver asked, noticing his friend's happiness. "You okay?"

Jim chuckled, still feeling lightheaded.

"Let's see them deny my Admiralty when I have my own fleet."

"Huh?" Oliver said, sitting forward. His eyes popped open. "You went to the Cortet house? Ha, she's going to get in so much trouble with her brother."

"I didn't know she had a brother," Jim said, confused. "She said she was an only child."

Oliver shook his head and waved a hand in the air. "Never mind. Forget I said that. Well, congratulations, my friend, on your upcoming marriage to the King's cousin," he proclaimed. Oliver grinned, then burst out laughing. He set his pipe on the table.

"What?" Jim demanded. "What's so funny?"

"Nothing, congratulations," Oliver replied, standing up and slapping Jim on the shoulder before walking past into the cockpit. "Just don't have high expectations for your wedding night."

Chapter 12
Sector 4 – Alderson
Jayson Coley

1

"It's been weeks," Alyssa bemoaned, standing in the doorway to Alexander's private quarters. He hated having her around and was thoroughly fed up with her; she was a spoiled child who was never properly disciplined and felt that the world owed her something.

Of course, he would never voice his concerns out loud. She was, for all intents and purposes, his boss, and he needed to keep her happy. Angering her would cause her to lash out, and even though he was certain Maven would defend him if anything dangerous came to light, he knew forcing Maven into that position would make her mad as well.

And that terrified him far more than dealing with Alyssa.

"The soldiers should be arriving today at the latest. We will be able to leave soon and camp near the research facility to watch everything unfold."

"Where are the four?"

"Still out in the woods."

"They should be back by now."

"They will not return until after the endeavor. We are to have no contact with them."

"I was to be allowed to see them," she argued. "I wanted to speak with them before this trial was undertaken."

"The message I received made it clear that they were to have no contact with anyone before the trial was underway to avoid contamination."

"They weren't to have contact with *Maven,*" Alyssa said.

Alexander stared at her, refusing to respond. Of course, that was what the message had dictated, but he had taken it one step further and completely separated them out. The last thing he wanted was for Alyssa to have access to them and cause problems. He had no doubt she would sabotage everything if she could.

Petulant child, he thought, careful to keep his face calm.

"You intentionally delayed the soldiers," Alyssa said. "They should have been here weeks earlier."

"The train was undergoing repairs," Alexander lied. "The delay was inevitable."

That was wholly untrue, but the delay was necessary. He was finding it difficult to separate himself from Alyssa. She watched him like a hawk, and he needed to gather supplies for his four soldiers before they reached the facility.

He couldn't trust anyone else with the task because Alyssa was questioning everyone she could find and making sure no one was disobeying the spirit of her little trial.

Technically, he couldn't give them any supplies...but, if they found items along the way, there was nothing he could do about that.

He wouldn't risk leaving weapons, though. That would be a step too far and could cause significant problems if Alyssa ever found out.

"The train wouldn't take weeks to repair," Alyssa said.

"It is an old train."

"Still, you could have hired more help to—"

"If you are accusing me of something," he said, speaking softly but with an edge of iron in his tone. "Then make your accusation, and be done with it. Don't dance around the issue."

Alyssa grimaced, furious with him. "Did my sister put you up to it? You are delaying on her behalf?"

"I haven't spoken to her in weeks."

"Yes, but you *know* what she expects of you."

"She expects me to oversee this friendly wager between the two of you. It is a friendly wager, is it not? A test of Maven's assets."

He knew from the look on her face that he'd backed her into a corner. She was constantly trying to downplay the stakes of the situation to try and demean Maven, but she was also desperate for the four to fail, which meant the pretense that this was a sisterly feud and nothing more.

If she were to admit that it was something more, it would reframe the entire situation and cast her in an unfavorable light. Alexander hated the machinations and underhanded lying that rich and powerful people undertook, but he certainly understood the game.

"Of course," she said. "But the rules were laid out by Darius himself."

"And they are being followed accordingly," Alexander replied. "I have had no contact with any of the four, and they know nothing about what they will face. They have no weapons or supplies and will move out as soon as the soldiers have arrived. Is this not the case?"

She wanted to call his bluff. He could see it plainly on her face, but she knew better. Instead, she turned on her heels and left his chambers, leaving him alone once more.

He watched her go and then let out a long sigh. Maven had been keeping away from the area, making sure that there was no way Alyssa could cry foul in the situation, but she would be arriving with the soldiers in the next few days.

He looked forward to getting this over with. The sooner he was able to be rid of Alyssa, the better.

2

As soon as he woke up, Jayson's eyes shot open. He didn't move, didn't even budge from his sleeping position near the campfire. He knew immediately that something was wrong, and they weren't alone in the camp.

Another test? He wasn't sure, but he could feel something in the air. A presence around them. Someone, or something, was watching them. He couldn't see or hear anything, but he would wager his life on being correct.

After a few seconds, he heard the relaxed snoring of Richard, asleep on the other side of the campfire. His breathing was calm and steady, nothing out of the ordinary, so he doubted Richard had noticed that anything was wrong.

He didn't get up, but he did shift ever so slightly so that he was in closer reach of his makeshift weapons. All he had right now was a spear he'd sharpened, but it would be enough to keep him safe from any local wildlife.

More seconds ticked past. He listened to Richard's breathing and watched the area around them, taking deep and steady breaths to make it seem like he was sleeping. It was quiet, but he didn't allow himself to relax. Not yet.

He heard a scuffing sound from outside camp. Someone was hiding out there, maybe fifteen meters away, he was sure of it now. He listened, straining to hear another movement, and then he heard more shifting steps as someone approached their camp.

Two people, he realized, and they were moving in on Richard's side. His friend was still asleep, still snoring. The footsteps stopped, still about ten meters from the campfire.

"Only one is sleeping," a familiar voice said.

Jayson relaxed and climbed slowly to his feet. Two people were waiting just outside the camp: Tricia Jester and Bret Finnegan.

"I was wondering when you guys might show up."

Tricia nodded at him. "We were told to come find you."

"By who? Alexander?"

"No," Bret said. "Not exactly. We woke up a few days ago and found a note in our camp. It just said: *East.*"

"How long have we been out here?" Jayson asked.

Bret shrugged. "Lost count of the days. Around three weeks?"

Jayson stepped forward and kicked Richard lightly on the shoulder. Richard snorted and groaned, rolling shakily to his feet and awkwardly trying to defend himself.

"Wha...?" he mumbled.

He saw Tricia and instantly relaxed. "Trish," he said.

She nodded at him. He rushed over and wrapped her in a hug, kissing her. She seemed surprised but didn't pull away from his embrace.

"I didn't think I could survive another day without you," he said. "I haven't been able to sleep when you aren't around."

"You seemed to be sleeping just fine," she replied.

"A fluke," he explained, winking at Jayson. "Ask Jayson. I haven't slept at all before tonight."

Jayson sighed. "So what do we do now?"

"No idea," Bret said. "But we were sent here to find you, so I'm assuming they want us to stick together. How are you on supplies?"

"Not a lot of what they originally gave us left," Jayson said. "We've been hunting and built up a small shelter, but we assumed we wouldn't be out here forever. We have some meat and vegetables stockpiled. What about you?"

"We only brought light provisions with us to find you. Our camp was considerably more...developed."

Jayson chose not to view the statement as an insult.

"Do you think we should keep moving?"

Tricia chimed in, "No. I think we were sent here to find you. And we have. If Alexander wants us to do something else, then he'll tell us."

"I agree," Bret said. "Plus, we've been walking all night and I could use some rest. It was much easier to follow the smoke of your campfire than track you during the day."

Jayson dug into their stockpiles and put together a small meal and then the four of them sat around the fire. Tricia and Richard sat together leaning against a log, resting on each other.

It was peaceful just eating their meal in silence. Jayson had to admit it felt good finally seeing some other people out here. He knew, however, that this meant that whatever they were out here to do, it was nearly time.

"What do you think this mission is?" Bret asked. "It can't be as simple as clearing out an old research facility."

"What else do you think it might be?"

"An ambush, maybe. This could be a test. What do you think?"

"No clue," Jayson said. "I'm just ready to get it over with."

"Alexander doesn't seem to have much faith in us making it through it."

"I think he's just blowing smoke," Richard said. "He likes to exaggerate and make stuff up."

"Are we talking about the same man?" Bret asked. "He's the most straightforward person I've ever met."

"I don't think we have to worry about it," Tricia said. "Until we know more, there is no sense in wasting time thinking about it."

The next morning they found another note pinned to a tree near them. None of them had heard anything or anyone come into their camp during the night.

It said one word: *North.*

3

"I didn't realize heading north would be so crappy," Richard said.

They had been hiking for the last four days, and it was starting to get bitterly cold. None of them had prepared for a trek like this, but after a day of hiking, they had come across bags of supplies that had everything they needed, including food, water, and cold weather clothing and equipment.

No weapons, though.

"Alderson is known for extreme weather patterns," Tricia replied. "It fluctuates wildly over short distances. That's part of why they weren't willing to build major cities here. It's simply too dangerous."

The supplies had also included climbing gear, but the ground was relatively level and they hadn't needed it yet. He had confidence, though, that Alexander wouldn't have packed it for them if it wasn't necessary.

For Jayson, this was a tremendous relief. He was stiff and tired from just sitting around and doing nothing for the last several weeks, so the chance to move around was incredibly rewarding.

"Still, you would think they would give us some idea of why we were hiking through the middle of a frozen tundra," Richard said. "Why can't they send us to a nice secluded beach with eighty-degree weather?"

"Does he ever shut up?" Bret asked.

"Never," Jayson said.

"Nope," Richard agreed. "I talk when I'm bored and when I'm tired, and right now I'm both, so you might as well get used to it."

4

It continued like that for another two days' worth of hiking, the temperature gradually dipping and the landscape becoming more and more unforgiving. The night came on faster and faster, but they couldn't afford to travel in the darkness. The possibility of slipping and falling into a ravine or into a hole was simply too great.

They finally found uses for their climbing gear on that second day and were forced to scale up and down cliff faces that were icy and sheer. It was something they'd done before, though, so it wasn't too difficult and they were still able to make good time.

He wasn't exactly sure where they were going. He knew they should be on the lookout for a research facility, but he didn't know what to expect: Would it be built into the side of a mountain or a standalone structure? Was it low in the valley or high on one of the cliffs? He was afraid that if they happened to be a few degrees off in their trek, they might simply miss it and walk right past.

When they found what they were looking for, however, it was obvious they had made it to the right place.

The facility was enormous. It stretched out in a canyon in front of them, at least a kilometer in diameter and several stories tall, a dome structure concealing whatever actual facility was beneath. It looked old, at least a few hundred years, and was packed in snow and ice on most of the exterior. Enormous spires and towers climbed into the clouds from out of the structure with large cylindrical dishes attached to them.

"What the hell is that?" Bret asked.

"Looks like a small city," Jayson said.

"I didn't think there was anything like that out here."

"It's the research facility," Tricia said. "Looks like it was abandoned a long time ago. I don't see any tracks nearby, even from animals."

"We're here to clear it out, right? There must be something inside."

"There certainly must be," Tricia said. "It's almost nightfall. We should camp here and start again in the morning."

"Why? We're almost there and we have a few hours of light left."

"We don't know if the facility has power. Do you see those glass sections? They let light in, and no doubt that will be the only light we have. I'd rather not go in and then find out its pitch black inside."

"Fair enough," Jayson said.

They set up camp, using snow to build a shelter against the wind and then huddling together to stay warm. Jayson watched the dome, fascinated by it. It could easily house thousands of people living comfortably and had been built to withstand time and elements.

"Why do you think they abandoned it?" he asked.

"No doubt practicality," Bret said. "When the Academy closed down and the Republic abandoned the planet, they probably had no more use for it."

"Still, the place probably cost a fortune," Jayson said. "You would think people would come live here if they abandoned it."

"It's a long way from anything important," Bret replied.

"Still...I bet a community could survive out here without much trouble just using the tools left behind."

"Maybe," Bret said. "You think there's another reason?"

"We're out here to clear the place out. Maybe whatever else is living there is way worse than what we're imagining."

Bret was silent for a long moment. "That's a scary thought."

Chapter 13
Sector 6 – Jaril
Oliver Atchison

1

Oliver watched his friend disappear into the garishly decorated hover car with his new bride, waving at the wedding guests who cheered them on. Jim was smiling. Oliver tried to think back to another time he'd seen his friend so happy and realized he couldn't. Jim Crater might be entering into a sham marriage, but he was thrilled about it.

And why wouldn't he be? He was getting what he really wanted, which was a new fleet of Galleon Class starships. They were old, bulky and poorly designed, but they flew. Right now the crews were at half capacity, which meant Jim would be able to hire on virtually anyone he wanted to build his own naval force. Jim had already put Oliver in charge of half of the fleet and taken the largest vessel as his flagship.

But even that paled in comparison to everything else that had happened in the preceding three months. Ever since Margaret Cortet announced the upcoming marriage and support for Admiral Jim Crater, they had been receiving daily requests for other ships to join their fleet. It seemed that now, when things were on the rise, everyone wanted to be involved in the new Admiral's business. People that would have laughed—and did—at Jim nine months ago were pledging ships and a lifetime of support. For many, it was their second pledged lifetime.

It had taken Oliver a few days to convince Jim to let him handle the negotiations. They would be tricky at best, and having an angry man in the mix wouldn't help anyone. Jim's gut reaction was to blow those merchants and nobles off for making a mockery of him before the sudden turn of events.

What would he want their support for? They had proven themselves unreliable manipulators at best, struggling to upend his operation. But finally Jim had acquiesced and Oliver was left to negotiate with the nobles and bureaucrats. Now their small fleet was growing almost daily. It was already numbering at forty warships and a combined crew of almost nineteen thousand men and women.

Oliver was thrilled about the turn of events. Now he held a seat of power on the third most powerful fleet in the Indeil Kingdoms. They couldn't begin to compete with the other Admirals militarily, but that didn't matter. The other Admirals had no interest in taking jobs for profit, feeling it was a lesser endeavor left to lowlifes and scum.

Oliver, with Jim's blessing, was already setting up their ships on weekly trading routes, moving goods. He'd even begun picking at his contacts in Terminus to try and set up long term trade deals that could make a fortune. Suddenly, his business possibilities seemed only limited by his imagination.

The thought made Oliver smile. He had quite the imagination.

Now that the bride and groom were off on their honeymoon—Oliver was mildly curious what that would entail...evidently Margaret had spoken of a desire to have children, though perhaps through a surrogate—the party quickly dispersed.

People headed for their own hover cars while a crew of sixty went about the business of cleaning up. Oliver made his way toward the exit, pulling his pipe out of his pocket and struggling to ignore his own depression.

Elizabeth had been at the party as one of the bridesmaids, looking elegant and wonderful in a silken green dress that matched the bride's hair. Unfortunately, her brother was also at the wedding, and she had no choice but to leave as a member of his entourage. She'd had no problem, he noted, pretending he was a bug underfoot.

The thought made him bitter, and he tried to remind himself that he didn't love her anyway.

You were never good at lying to yourself, part of him whispered. That *same* part told him that Elizabeth would be the only woman he loved from this point forth. He knew that she had some feelings for

128

him, but he couldn't imagine a way of making the relationship last. At least not with Hektor Menschen in the picture. Oh, how he hated that man. *I'd kill him, if it would let me have his sister...*

Instead he offered the advice of making Hektor groomsman. Politically it was a brilliant move. The offer was a powerful gesture of mending fences and building alliances. Yet he wasn't disappointed when Jim refused. There were some fences that could stay broken.

At least Jim had been willing to deal with the other Admiral. Brutus Volt had never really objected to Jim's position. He was a quiet man, older and more seasoned. He avoided politics like the plague. Oliver convinced Jim to make Brutus his best man. Jim tried to refuse Brutus, as well. Best man, Jim claimed, belonged to Oliver and Oliver alone.

But Oliver had been insistent. This was the time to create bonds of friendship that would last a lifetime, and offering the position of best man to Brutus was a generous offer.

And Brutus clearly appreciated the honor. He gave Jim an expensive wedding gift: an Urca Class starship; a huge hulking behemoth incapable of fighting but with triple the cargo space of any other ship they had.

Oliver paused at the exit of the enormous auditorium, aware that someone was watching him. It was a short man with scrawny arms and legs and a big belly sitting at a table on the other side of the hall. He beckoned for Oliver to join him.

"What's this now?" Oliver mumbled softly, walking across the hall.

The lights dimmed in the hall, casting them in gloom.

The cleaning crews were making the rounds, but otherwise the place was empty. There were still enough people that Oliver doubted he was in danger, but he had a butterfly knife in his pocket nonetheless.

His solid-bottomed boots clicked against the auditorium floor as he strode to the table. He sat down without acknowledging the other man and lit his pipe. The building was virtually covered with *no smoking* signs. Oliver had a habit of ignoring those signs. He was a member of the upper echelon now. Such signs didn't apply to him.

Or at least that's what he told himself. In either case, no one ever brought it up. He inhaled a puff of tobacco and sized up the man sitting opposite him. He wore an expensive suit, but the pants hung too low around the ankles while the sleeves were too short. *A rental.* Definitely not sized properly. Up close, he seemed nervous and out of sorts, refusing to make eye contact. *Not a noble.*

Oliver scanned his memory of the invitation list. The security teams were diligent, so no one whose name wasn't on that list could get in. Most guests were either part of the Royal Family or close friends, which meant there were only three people who weren't noble born—excepting himself and Jim, of course. One guest he knew well from his time on the streets, and another was a woman. That left one possibility.

"Antonio Rolins," Oliver said, leaning back in the chair and crossing his leg at the knee. The man made no move, but the tensing at his shoulders made it clear Oliver was correct.

"Have we met? You must have an excellent memory," the man said softly.

No, and my memory isn't very good either. But I am very, very good at what I do, Oliver thought. Out loud: "To what do I owe the pleasure?"

"I was asked to give you something," the man explained, pulling a data pad out of his pocket. He passed it across the table to Oliver. "I represent a man named Victor Foley. Vic for short." Oliver set his pipe between his teeth and scrolled through the images.

"What am I looking at?" he asked through his teeth.

"The first three images are of a meeting between Sir Rodrik Fulk and another man at Sir Rodrik's estate on Geid. The other images are from a luncheon those same men had three days ago on Immis. Sir Rodrik showed up to the meal in disguise. The other man, we've learned, is a member of the Planetary Union."

Oliver set the data pad on the table. "I'm assuming you have another reason to hinder my sleep than to show me a few pictures," he said.

His unaffected attitude had the desired response, putting the man further off guard. Antonio *had* come here specifically to show Oliver those pictures, but the conversation wasn't going how he intended.

The images did bother Oliver, but he wasn't about to admit that. Not yet at least. He had a fairly good idea why this man was here, but he didn't want to allow an assumption to sneak up and bite him in the ass. There were too many times in the past that had happened.

130

"They...um...the Union is trying to...invade..." Antonio struggled for words.

"Invade a diner?" Oliver asked, adding a note of incredulity to his voice. "In fact, I think I recognize it as Freemont's Café," he added, picking the data pad up and scrolling to a particular image. "If they do invade, we can only hope they kill the baker."

"Please take the...uh...data pad to Mr. uh...Sir Crater," Antonio mumbled, standing up. "We have begun forming a resistance movement to keep the Union out of our kingdom, but..."

"You need money," Oliver finished for him. The man hesitated and then nodded firmly, regaining some confidence.

"Yes, we need money. And from everything I've heard, Jim Crater is quite sympathetic to our cause."

Oliver waved his hand dismissively and stood up. "Different times my friend. It's one thing to run warships out of our system and quite another to spend money needlessly against a never-ending conspiracy." Oliver picked up the data pad and slipped it into his pocket, then offered his hand to the man. "But you have my word that the information will make it to my friend."

The man shook his hand and reached into his jacket pocket, trembling slightly. "Well if he decides to uh...we will call you in a few days—"

"If we decide anything, we will contact you," Oliver affirmed, his tone making it clear that there would be no debate on the issue. The man looked like he wanted to object—it was clearly not the parameters he was sent to negotiate—but he didn't dare to.

Oliver nodded to the man and strode out of the auditorium. He felt more than a little annoyed by the entire situation.

He'd been expecting something to happen. The Union had shifted tactics in the last two years. They didn't return with warships, but a number of tradesman had shown up on the planet with unheard-of weapons and trinkets. Oliver hadn't signed any deals with them—the Royal Family declared anyone who did a traitor, and he couldn't afford to get caught—but he knew it was a thriving business. And it would only grow. People could say what they wanted about national pride, but everyone had a selling point.

But he was a little bothered that it was happening so quickly.

He would have to look into the details before passing the message on to Jim, but he was already sure what the truth of the matter was: The Union was biding its time for another big push, and the Royal Family wouldn't stand up to them. Jim would, though. Hell, he might ask to *run* the resistance group.

Oliver sighed. He might as well start making plans for it in the budget.

Chapter 14
Sector 6 – Eldun
Vivian Drowel

1

Vivian woke Traq up early the next morning, hoping to make it to Delphi and onto their ship, *Junker*, before they had to seek shelter again. She knew from the previous night and seeing the scouts from the city that they weren't far from their final destination.

She also knew that the army from Briden's Ward wouldn't be far off either. She hadn't seen their scouts the previous day, so she had to hope that maybe she had enough of a lead to get her and Traq to safety. The war was coming, and it would be bloody if the past was any indication. She didn't want to be caught in the middle of it.

Traq had recovered fairly well from the previous few days of strenuous hiking and seemed to be in high spirits. They stayed out of sight in the abandoned city while eating their breakfast. He was also extremely hungry, shoveling food into his mouth with abandon.

"Are you ready to go, Traq?" she asked, checking the street one last time while he packed his bags.

"Uh huh," he said, shouldering it and grinning at her.

She couldn't believe how fast his body had recovered from their last few days of hiking, but she wasn't about to complain about small favors. She nodded at him, held her finger to her lips to signal for him to stay quiet, and started trekking back out of the destroyed city.

Once they made it back into the forest, she realized they were probably safe once again and allowed herself to relax. It would only be another couple of kilometers back to Delphi, and she was starting to feel that they were in the clear.

They had also managed to make the trek in about half the time she'd accounted for. It wasn't quite the relaxing vacation she had been hoping for, but it was turning out to be an excellent trip in other ways.

"Are we almost back to the city?" Traq asked after a few hours of hiking. He spoke louder than she would have liked, but she decided not to berate him for it. After all, it was a beautiful day out, sunny and bright.

"Almost there," Vivian replied. "We're almost out of this."

2

They were making a good pace, trekking through the forest in a direct line to their destination. She was doing her best to keep them in the thicker areas of the surrounding woods, hoping there wouldn't be any drones in the area to report their position to either army.

It was a hot day, and after the last few, they were running low on water. She had a purifier on hand to refill their jugs, but they hadn't come across any streams or rivers yet. They were rationing, but they would both start feeling the effects if she wasn't careful. She made sure to give him extra water, not wanting him to start slipping into the quiet exhaustion he'd experienced over the last few days.

She knew they were close to Delphi now. Each step was getting more and more dangerous. Part of her wished she'd grabbed a gun or two from the scouts she had knocked unconscious. It would have made her seem like a greater threat, she knew, and they would be hunting her down now, but it would have been worth it just to have some sort of defense to keep them both safe.

3

Around midday, Traq grabbed her arm and stopped walking. It was quiet in the woods around them, and she tensed up when he touched her. She glanced at him, confused, and saw a look of terror on his face.

She didn't hesitate, knowing better than to ignore his instincts. She quickly looked for cover and found a copse of trees they could hide inside. It was painful moving through the brush but kept them out of anyone's line of sight.

Once they were safely out of sight, she raised an eyebrow at Traq, silently asking him why they had stopped. As far as she could tell, there was nothing around them anywhere nearby.

He pointed forward in the direction they had been walking, but she couldn't see or hear anything. Maybe this time he hadn't been right, and there was nothing there. Still, she waited a few extra minutes, and then she heard the rustling sound of movement up ahead.

The sound grew as a group of soldiers moved through the foliage toward them. They were all in heavy armor and armed to the teeth. She watched as about thirty of them moved in their direction.

Vivian watched them approach, ducking down and shaking her head silently. She would have seen them approaching in time to get her and Traq out of sight without much of an issue: the soldiers weren't even hiding their presence in the forest.

What shocked her was how *quickly* Traq had noticed them. He knew they were there long before they were in earshot or visible through the trees, which meant something else had tipped him off to their presence.

Much the same, she realized, as what had tipped him off to the group of scouts earlier. She knew without a doubt now that he was manifesting some sort of ability. She simply wished she knew more about what it was.

The soldiers passed by their hiding place, heading farther north, completely oblivious to their presence. Vivian could tell Traq was terrified seeing them up close, and she held his hand while they walked past to keep him calm.

Once the soldiers were past, she helped Traq climb back out of the hiding place.

"You knew they were there like the ones from last night?"

"Yeah. I just...knew."

She stared at him for a second and then nodded. It seemed that the longer he was out here, and the more dangerous the situation, the more powerful he became. She didn't even think Argus would have been able to sense a moving band like that from so far away, and that was with his implant.

But she couldn't delve into it right now. They didn't have time. She got Traq moving again, and they headed back onto their course toward Delphi.

About twenty minutes later, they came across a stream. Traq was staggering along now, exhausted, so she decided this would be the perfect opportunity to take a break. Part of her wanted to refill their bottles and press on, but she knew Traq wouldn't be able to keep moving much longer and they were getting close to the city. She needed him at his best when they arrived at Delphi.

She found some rocks for them to sit on near a little waterfall and they took a break. Her legs were weary, but Traq had it worse. He was asleep in only a couple of minutes. She knew he was at his breaking point. They listened to the babbling brook for a while in silence.

She decided to let Traq rest for a couple of hours and took the time to meditate. Her head was still sore from using her implant, but she was afraid she might need to use it again before they reached the safety of Delphi.

4

They were back moving after about an hour's rest. Traq was limping now, barely able to keep his feet and having lost the energy he had this morning, but she didn't have a lot of options. She considered carrying him, but knew she needed to keep her own strength up as well in case they ran into any hostile situations.

She wasn't making as good of time as she'd hoped and was afraid they would need to stop for another night before making it to their ship. They were too close to the city for her to rest comfortably, but she didn't want to keep Traq going in the middle of the night and risk him hurting himself.

Her concerns proved well founded as night fell. The city lights were off in the distance, still several kilometers away. She was looking for a place to stop for the night and rest when she heard voices in the distance coming toward them.

She started to look for a hiding place when she heard one of them shout, "Halt!"

Her exhaustion was getting the best of her, she knew. These were Delphi soldiers out patrolling the area in anticipation of the oncoming army, and she'd walked right up to them. She should have seen them coming or expected them.

Too late to worry about that now. She put her body between Traq and the guns and held up her hands.

"We mean you no harm," she said.

"Declare yourself," a man said, rifle still raised.

"We are civilians heading to Delphi. I am a diplomat on behalf of the Republic."

"Delphi is closed to outsiders."

"Bring us to General Coley and he will explain. We have immunity and need to get off world before the army arrives."

"The gates are closed to everyone right now. The general is busy and not to be bothered."

Vivian had been afraid something like that would happen, but there was nothing she could really do about it. She still needed to get to her ship one way or another.

"We are trying to retrieve our ship and get off world."

"Your ship?"

"It is docked in the city."

"If that is true, then your ship has already been seized as contribution to the war effort."

Vivian had assumed as much. It was a valuable item, especially in a time of war like this, and there was nothing like martial law and fear to seize assets and line the government's coffers with funds.

There was no way they'd sold the ship yet, however, and she was certain that it was still locked up and ignored for now in the same place where she had left it. It would take them time to crack the security and they had other things to worry about than confiscating her ship.

"In either case, we need to—"

"You need to turn around and leave," the soldier said, gesturing at her with his gun.

"There is an army behind us."

"That isn't our concern. You will not gain entry to Delphi, nor will we escort you out of this territory."

Vivian sighed. "I have a child with me."

"Then you shouldn't have brought him here."

The finality of the statement sunk in. She knew the man was right, and on a deeper level than she would have anticipated. She never should have brought Traq out here, and all she'd managed to do was put him at risk and possibly get him killed.

And for what? Some useless venture out into the woods to test him? She already knew he was an amazing child with a lot of potential, and she didn't need to be on a war-torn planet to see that.

She seemed to be really good at making mistakes like this.

Vivian bowed her head, focusing on the implant, and then lashed out. All six guns jerked up, aiming high over her head. She heard a few grunts and gasps of surprise as the soldiers fought back, trying to maintain control over their weapons.

She leapt forward, kicking the speaking soldier in the diaphragm and then punching him in the throat. He collapsed to the ground with a grunt.

Another soldier pulled the trigger on his gun, firing off rounds into the sky. The sound was loud and echoed, probably warning anyone else in the area of their presence, but she didn't have time to worry about it now. She stepped to another soldier and swept the woman's leg, tripping her to the ground. She hit the dirt, and Vivian kicked her in the throat.

The soldier that was firing bullets into the sky jerked against his gun, pulling the trigger again and again. Another soldier yanked at his own weapon, releasing the grip and grabbing the barrel itself.

Another woman dropped her gun and charged at Vivian, drawing a dagger and launching a kick at Vivian's head. Vivian caught her leg and swung her to the side, slamming her into a tree. She hit hard with a grunt and then dropped to the ground. Vivian stomped on her stomach and then kicked her in the face.

She heard a sound behind her and ducked. A wild punch flew over her back. She pivoted and launched an uppercut, hitting the attacker in the chin. He staggered to the side, then came back with a series of blows.

Vivian deflected and backpedaled. More shots were fired, and she felt her control over the guns wavering as the two soldiers continued trying to jerk their weapons free of her mental grip.

Her current attacker kicked and punched, forcing her to give ground and move back. The strain was too much, and she lost control over the weapons. She saw four of them fall out of the sky from the corner of her eye, bouncing on the ground. The last two came loose in the grips of the two men who were still holding onto them.

138

She lashed out with her mind, hitting the man holding the barrel of his gun and throwing him into the tree. The distraction caused her to take a solid punch to the upper eye from her attacker, followed by a knee to the stomach, but she somehow managed to keep her feet.

The other man who had been firing into the sky seemed almost surprised to have control of his gun once more. He looked at it in awe for a second and then turned toward Vivian, sighting in at her. He squeezed the trigger, but his clip was empty. He growled in frustration.

Vivian focused on the man coming at her now, knowing she was running out of time. She deflected a series of attacks, dropped low under a wild swing and then launched a flurry of punches of her own. Her hits landed, first in his kidney and then his jaw. He stumbled back and she rushed after, kicking him in the shin and then the upper thigh.

He stumbled farther, trying to dodge back, but she didn't give him time to recover. She kneed him in the chin and then punched him in the throat. As he fell to the ground, she gave him a last kick, making sure he stayed down.

Then she turned back to itchy-fingers. He had grabbed a partner's weapon and was raising it toward her, ready to fire once more.

The distance was too great for her to close in on him. She reached out mentally with her implant, but by the time she summoned the energy to deflect his gun away from her, it would be too late.

She stepped forward just as he pulled the trigger. The sound of a barking gunshot filled the area. She closed her eyes, waiting to feel the bullet pierce her.

But it didn't.

Everything...froze.

She opened her eyes, and they focused on a speck in front of her. She saw that it was a bullet hovering in the air only a few centimeters in front of her face. She stepped to the side, staring at it in muted fascination. Ahead of her, the soldier was locked in position, gun to his shoulder and standing perfectly still.

The only part of him that was moving were his eyes, and they were full of confusion and terror as he strained to move his body.

It took Vivian a long few seconds to understand what was happening. She looked to the side and saw Traq standing there, face a mask of concentration and hands held up in front of him like he was conducting an orchestra. His entire body was shaking he was so tense.

Vivian felt her jaw drop open and then reminded herself the fight wasn't over. The soldier was paralyzed, not out of commission. Vivian rushed forward, grabbed a stone off the ground, and bashed him in the side of the head with it.

He fell to the ground, unconscious. Suddenly there was a thud as the bullet smashed into a tree twenty or so meters behind her, and she heard Traq start gasping. She rushed over to him and saw that his eyes were bloodshot. Veins had popped out on his arms and legs, and he was still shaking. He started to stumble.

"Traq!" she said, catching him and holding him up for inspection. He was groggy and dazed.

"I'm okay," he mumbled, the words running together. "Is it over?"

"Yeah," she said.

He closed his eyes, still panting, and nodded. After about thirty seconds, he opened them again, and he looked mostly recovered.

"Are you sure you're okay?" she asked.

He nodded. "I think so."

"How did you...?" she asked, not even sure how to phrase the question.

He hesitated. "I *felt* you do it," he explained.

"What do you mean *felt*?" she said, confused.

He frowned and shook his head. "I don't know. You grabbed their guns with your mind, and I felt you do it, so I did the same thing."

Except it wasn't the same thing. She had deflected guns, inanimate objects. Traq had stopped a man completely, paralyzed him, and he had also stopped a bullet in mid-flight. Both of those things were nearly impossible feats, even for someone who trained for years to do that exact thing.

To do both at the same time, and without any training, was unthinkable. She'd never heard of a single Shield doing something like that, even with an implant.

"Thank you," she said awkwardly, helping him find his footing.

"Of course," he said. "Do you think we should keep moving?"

"Yeah, we need to keep going forward," she said.

Her mind ached with a massive headache, keeping her from focusing on anything for too long, but she knew that as soon as they settled down to rest, she would have to deal with what she'd just watched happen.

Chapter 15
Sector 1 – Axis
Abdullah Al Hakir

1

Abdullah lay back on the cot in his spartan chambers and rubbed his face, trying to come to terms with everything that had happened in the last few weeks. His bed was basically just a rigid board built up against the wall, the kind he'd grown used to in his years of being a common soldier.

The original bed for the First Officer was plush, soft, and entirely miserable to try and sleep on. He'd replaced it in the first few days after being promoted when his back began hurting. He'd never looked back.

He'd also replaced the desk—the old one took up too much space—and given away a lot of rugs and paintings that the previous First Officer had collected. He liked to have as much open area in his quarters as possible to give himself room to think. Nothing in here was a waste of space or distraction.

Right now, though, he felt he could do with a little bit of distraction. He was exhausted but couldn't sleep, and he hadn't managed to relax since Captain Grove had first put him in charge of the trial.

He couldn't get his mind to stop spinning and thinking through worst-case scenarios. He'd been expecting a day like this to crop up ever since his promotion, where he was finally in over his head, but so far he'd been lucky. Something crappy was bound to happen.

To be honest, he was amazed he'd managed to survive this long as First Officer without things going off the rails. But now that they had, he understood the weight that was on his shoulders. He had a terrible decision to make, and it was important that he got it right.

2

Eddie Boleman showed up a few hours later to give his daily status report. Abdullah had advised him to update him each afternoon about all of the evidence that had come up in the trial.

To be honest, nothing had changed after the first few days. The evidence was incredibly cut and dry, and there was no disputing what the soldier had done. It was an unforgivable crime, and he'd been caught virtually in the act of doing it.

Eddie still showed up every day, but Abdullah was fairly sure it was to check on him and make sure he was okay more than to fill him in on the developments in the evidence gathering. Abdullah appreciated that.

"How are you doing?" Eddie asked as he came into Abdullah's chambers. He took a seat at Abdullah's desk and looked quizzically at his friend.

"Fine, I think," Abdullah said.

"You look exhausted."

"I am. The Captain is getting antsy. She expected me to give my decision a few weeks ago. I know she isn't happy that I'm taking this long."

"She wants you to execute Gregory?"

"She's never said what she wants me to do. Whenever I ask, she deflects."

"Yeah, but..."

He didn't bother to finish the sentiment, and he didn't have to. They both knew—as did every other soldier aboard the ship—that the Captain would have executed the Ensign immediately for the crime, probably before the evidence was even gathered proving his guilt.

"So what are you going to do?" Eddie asked.

"I don't know," Abdullah said, shaking his head. "There are some parts of this that just don't add up."

"What do you mean?"

144

"The reports."

"Again?" Eddie asked, a touch of annoyance in his voice. "We've been over this."

"It still doesn't make sense. There was a restraining order on Gregory. He'd been stalking her for months, and orders were to keep them apart."

"And the system made a mistake. They got paired up on duty."

"How, though? There were strict parameters in place to keep them apart."

"The system messed up."

"Did it? I'm not so sure."

"What do you mean?"

"What if someone intentionally paired them up?"

"What? Who would do something like that?"

"I don't know. But what if they did?"

"They didn't. We went through the logs, remember? No one tampered with it."

"Logs can be faked."

"Seems like a lot of effort for someone to go through, and for what? To put the girl in the same room alone with her unstable stalker?"

"Isn't it possible?"

"No," Eddie said flatly. "And even if it was, it is still meaningless."

"What do you mean?"

"The restraining order wasn't to protect *him*, it was to protect her. You're looking at this as though someone set him up, but what happened to *her* is the situation we are facing. Even if the two of them were paired together, he still had no right to do what he did."

"Yeah, but—"

"There are no buts here," Eddie said, cutting him off. "This isn't a 'what if' scenario. It happened. It doesn't matter how or why it happened, but now you have to decide what we are going to do about it."

Abdullah hesitated. "What would you do?"

"Kill him," Eddie replied bluntly. He didn't even stop to think about it. "We don't need people like him on this ship. There is a victim in this situation, and it isn't Gregory Tillman."

Abdullah didn't reply. He wished he could have Eddie's conviction, that complete belief that he was doing the right thing no matter what. For Eddie, this entire process was cut and dry, completely simple.

But there was nothing simple about it for Abdullah, and if Gregory was sentenced to death and executed, it would be Abdullah making that decision and not Eddie. He greatly respected his friend's opinion, but Eddie wasn't the one holding a man's fate and future in the balance.

"Thank you, Eddie, for stopping by," he said.

Eddie nodded. "No worries. I'll come back tomorrow to check on you and let you know if something else comes up."

Abdullah nodded at him but didn't reply. Eddie headed out into the hall, smiling at him before closing it, leaving Abdullah alone in his chambers once more. Alone, except for his thoughts.

He went back to the bed and lay down, hoping he might get some sleep but knowing he wouldn't.

3

There was a chime at his door about fifteen minutes after Eddie left. He wondered if maybe Eddie had forgotten something and come back. He sat up, folding his right knee up to his chest and running his left hand across the stubble of hair on his scalp. It was slick with sweat, even though the room was frigid.

"Come in," he said.

The door slid open.

Abigail Wade ran into the room, a giant grin on her face. She was cute with a round face and bright eyes, and it warmed his heart every time he saw her. That hadn't been as often as he would have liked over these last two years, and he couldn't help but think that she was growing up too fast.

It was like a breath of fresh air, and he found himself feeling better the second he saw her, like a weight had been lifted off of his shoulders.

"Dulah!" she shouted, jumping up onto his bed and throwing her little arms around his neck. Her hair was pulled back into a tight ponytail with a red ribbon to hold it in place. She was wearing a blue blouse that matched her eyes.

He chuckled, hugging her back and closing his eyes.

146

"Hey, Abi," he said. "What are you doing?"

"We came to bring you some food," Jamir Paskin said, stepping into the room behind her.

He was carrying a large tray loaded with several plates and a bowl of food, a pitcher that sloshed with each step he took, and a few cups. It was some sort of steamed vegetable platter with rice, and it smelled heavenly.

Jamir set the plate on his desk, spinning his chair around and sitting down.

"I'm not hungry," Abdullah said.

"Nonsense," Jamir said. "You haven't eaten anything in sixteen hours."

"You're tracking my eating habits?" Abdullah asked, more amused than angry.

It didn't surprise him. Nothing surprised him anymore where Captain Grove's personal servant was concerned. Jamir Paskin seemed to be everywhere and know everything that was going on. But never in a threatening or overbearing manner; rather, he was more nurturing. He was polite, intelligent, and friendly with everyone.

He was good with Abigail, as well, which Abdullah appreciated. He still felt terrible for the situation she'd been pushed into because of the Captain and Ministry, and he would never understand their decision. But at least he knew she was looked after.

"It's not a difficult supposition to make even without monitoring your intakes. You have a terrible decision to make, and you're worried about it. It upsets your indigestion and causes an imbalance in your blood sugar levels. We're just here to remedy that."

"You need sarton," Abi said with a definitive nod and grin.

"What?" Abdullah asked.

Jamir chuckled at her mispronunciation. "*Serotonin*," he corrected. "Tell Abdullah what we're learning right now."

"Algebra," she said. "And chemistry and anatomy. But I don't like anatomy. It's stupid."

"She prefers history," Jamir explained, "which is excellent, but mental agility and aptitude requires a basic understanding of various fields of study before self-selecting preferences."

"And tumbling!" Abi exclaimed.

Jamir smiled. "Yes, and tumbling."

"Do you want to see me do a roll?" Abi asked Abdullah. He looked at her skeptically.

"I don't think my room is big enough for gymnastics," he started to say.

Abigail ignored him. She was already on the floor, doing forward rolls across the metal. Abdullah looked at Jamir, who only shrugged.

Breathless, she climbed to her feet. "I can do cartwheels too!"

He held up his hand. "Maybe you can show me later. In fact, you can teach me if you want."

"Okay," she said, climbing back on the bed and sitting next to him. Jamir scooped the food onto plates and passed one to Abdullah and another to Abigail.

"The rice isn't special. It's three-month seed we grew to supplement our pantry. Serves better as sticky balls than in a dish like this, but it's all we have in stores. The vegetables, though, are from my personal garden."

"You have a garden?" Abdullah asked.

"In my quarters. Since I'm not an officer, I don't have access to the *Fist*'s stores of them."

"The Captain won't let you have any?"

He shook his head. "I wouldn't dare to ask. It would be improper of me to even suggest such impropriety on her part, or for her to offer me special treatment."

"I'd heard you don't eat meat."

"It's inefficient," Jamir explained. "Animal protein is difficult for our bodies to process without expending extra effort, so meat is an indulgence. When I indulge, my preference is for sweet treats. Right, Abi?"

"Right," Abi said through a mouthful of rice.

"She assists me in tending my garden," Jamir explained. "And we grow a tremendous variety of edible plants. She prepared this meal, in fact."

Abdullah turned his attention back to the plate. Some of the vegetables he recognized, but there were a few he didn't. One was a dark green leafy plant that tasted sour and another was a white stalk covered in tiny stems. It disintegrated into little strings when he bit into it, and the stems were rather tough and difficult to chew.

"It's delicious," he said, pushing the unknown vegetables to one side of his plate. He was careful that Abigail didn't see him do it.

148

Better to focus on the known foods for now, he decided.

"I agree," Abi said.

Only about half of the rice she scooped onto her fork made it into her mouth. The other half ended up on her blouse or his bed sheets.

Abdullah took a few more bites of the food, but his stomach was too off kilter to enjoy the flavors. It settled uncomfortably in his stomach, but he knew Jamir was right: he needed the calories to keep up his strength.

Either way, he was pleased by the distraction.

"Are you enjoying your classes?" Abdullah asked, setting his plate aside. He accepted an offered cup from Jamir. It was a sweet fruity drink laced with cinnamon.

"Uh huh."

"She has a good memory," Jamir said. "We've begun a little language study as well, but I haven't decided which languages would be best to teach her."

"Why teach her languages at all?" he asked. "Why not get her a translator?"

Abdullah had a universal translator implanted in his ear—standard issue for all officers—and with Abigail's position, it would be easy for her to get one as well. With it, she would be able to understand more than ninety percent of all spoken languages and dialects.

"Learning multiple languages is excellent for memory development," Jamir explained. "And helps with brain formation and adaptive skills. Memorizing scientific terminology, on the other hand, while necessary, isn't very fun."

"Force equals mass times acceleration," Abdullah said, sipping his drink. "That's pretty much all I remember from school."

Jamir smiled. "It's really all you need."

"What's that mean?" Abi asked, scrunching her nose. Abdullah laughed and rubbed the top of her head, messing up her hair.

"You'll find out later," Jamir replied, sipping his drink.

"I appreciate you coming," Abdullah added after a few more moments of silence. He didn't finish the thought, not wanting to kick them out, but he felt that their distraction would get in the way of the serious deliberation he needed to do.

"Absolutely our pleasure, but we should be going," Jamir said, fully understanding. He began gathering the plates and silverware onto his tray. "We have much to do."

"Of course."

"Abi, please go finish reading your chapter on nucleotides. I'll be along in a few minutes to quiz you about it."

"Okie dokie," Abi said, jumping up and giving Abdullah another hug. "Bye, Dulah!"

Then she disappeared out the door. Abdullah watched her go and then let out a sigh.

"Thanks," he said, turning to Jamir. "I needed a distraction."

Jamir nodded. "I know. If you need anything else?"

"What do you think I should do with this trial?"

"I'm not here to offer suggestions. Only comfort."

"What do you think I *will* do?" Abdullah asked. "You always seem to know."

"Of course, I know," Jamir said. "But telling you before you reach the requisite conclusions for yourself would defeat the entire purpose of this exercise. There is a necessary process to determinations like this. I'm here to ensure your body has the fuel necessary to think clearly so you can work through your predicament."

Abdullah leaned back on his cot, staring up at the ceiling. "Is it always going to be this difficult to make decisions like this?"

"The trick isn't making the decision," Jamir explained, scooping all of the food into the bowl and stacking the dishes to easily carry. He left them, though, and turned to focus on Abdullah. "You've already *made* up your mind about what you will do."

Abdullah sat up. "What?"

"You are the man you are," Jamir said, leaning back against the desk and crossing his arms over his large belly. "It's taken many years for you to become *this* man, so your virtues and beliefs aren't going to change at the whims of one problem."

"So you're saying I've already decided whether the Ensign lives or dies?"

"Of course, you have. You just haven't yet figured out *why* you made your choice. That will require understanding *who* you are, a significantly more difficult task than determining how you will act. But, once you have done that, you will know more about yourself."

"So you really think I've already made up my mind?" Abdullah surmised. "You're not just blowing smoke?

Jamir nodded. "You have, you're simply rebelling against it. Hindsight will be easier to navigate."

Abdullah let out a long sigh. "Can you give me a hint?"

Jamir smiled. "Very well, what did the man do?"

"You already know."

"Humor me."

"He sexually assaulted a young woman."

"What is his punishment?"

"That's what I need to decide."

"Yes, but there *are* recommended punishments for similar crimes, as well as precedent, correct?"

"But those run the gamut from a few months in prison to death."

"What do you feel is the proper punishment?"

Abdullah hesitated. "I don't know."

"Yes, you do," Jamir replied, shaking his head. "What would you expect to happen to you if you did something like that?"

"I wouldn't do something like that," Abdullah replied.

"Then use your imagination."

"I would expect death," Abdullah said. "But that is my own expectation. I hold myself to a higher standard than I hold others to."

"So, you feel that death is the proper punishment?"

"Yes," Abdullah said. "But I can't very well sentence a man to death because I *feel* like it's the right punishment, can I?"

"Why not," Jamir asked.

"Because..." Abdullah said, then trailed off. He held up his hands. "Because I'm in charge of this man's entire future and making a decision like this shouldn't be something I do because I *feel* like it."

"You should make your decision *exactly* because you feel like it," Jamir argued. "You *feel* like it because that is who you are. A million tiny decisions created the man standing before me and placed you in this position. If you spend too much time thinking about all of this, then of course you can find arguments against or for death. You are in the exact position you are in because of who you are, and that is the way you are meant to make this decision."

Abdullah looked down at his hands. "But what if I'm wrong?"

"Now you're asking if you are *fit* for the position," Jamir replied, "which is an entirely different question and not the one you are here to make."

"People can change. Maybe he deserves a second chance."

"Why?" Abdullah said.

"He could become a better person."

"There are millions of better people already. Billions, even."

"Now you sound like Eddie."

"He is a smart man. You picked him wisely to be your confidant. My point is, why spend so much time or resources on this one soldier?"

"Because every life is sacred."

"Do you truly believe that?" Jamir asked. "Is the life of a rapist sacred? A murderer? What about the people they hurt? Doesn't the family of such a person who committed *no* crime deserve vengeance?"

"So I should sentence him to death?"

"Should you?"

Abdullah sighed. "Damn it, Jamir."

"The purpose of a civilized society is to be above the petty desires of any one person. Alone we are weak, but together we can climb above concepts like vengeance and punishment. This should be about *justice*. Rape is a terrible crime, but is murder an apt punishment for it?"

"You are terrible at giving hints," Abdullah said.

Jamir bowed and picked up his tray. "This is something you need to discover for yourself. If you don't understand the decision you've made, then how are you going to be able to live with it?"

Abdullah rubbed his face. "I'm even more confused now than I was before you showed up. The Captain is expecting my answer in a few days at the latest, and she's already furious with me. And the only thing you can tell me is that I've already made up my mind. Oh, and that you can't tell me what it is."

"Another hint? Fine," Jamir said. Carrying his tray to the door. It slid open, but he hesitated in the threshold. "The soldier's name is Gregory Tillman."

Abdullah blinked. "Yeah, that's his name. So?"

Jamir turned slightly so that he could look Abdullah in the eyes. "When you spoke earlier, you referred to him by his rank. Ensign. You depersonalized him. Why would your subconscious mind do that in regards to a man you were about to pardon?"

152

Then Jamir stepped out the door. It slid shut behind him before Abdullah could respond. He sat alone on the cot, mulling the conversation over in his mind. It felt like a weight had been lifted off of his shoulders, and he could breathe again. And he had to admit that Jamir was right. The more he thought about it, the clearer the answer seemed to be:

In hindsight, it was the easiest decision in the world.

Chapter 16
Sector 4 – Alderson
Jayson Coley

1

They climbed down the cliff face the next morning to the structure below. It seemed quite a bit larger up close, and they were forced to walk another kilometer around the outside before they found an entrance they could use. It was a loading ramp designed for large vehicles to pass into the dome.

There was a several-thousand-pound reinforced door built for it, but it looked to have been busted open a long time ago; though whether it had been broken by explosives or...something else, they couldn't tell. Whatever it was, Jayson knew, it had to have been a pretty major event that had broken that metal monstrosity open.

They exchanged glances, but no one spoke up. They all knew there were quite a few large creatures living on this planet, but the idea that one of them had punched through the door was worrisome to say the least.

"After you," Richard said, gesturing for Jayson to go first.

He shrugged and headed into the building, and the rest quickly followed in after. It took a few moments for his eyesight to adjust to the darkness once they were inside. There were no lights on in the tunnel, or windows to allow any sunlight through.

The initial tunnel they walked into looked like an old underground roadway, sloping downward into darkness. Snow had drifted in through the new opening and covered much of the ground for the first few hundred meters, but after that, it actually grew warmer as they went deeper into the dome. It was eerily empty and grew darker and darker as they went.

They had a flashlight each as part of their equipment, but it did little to break through the heavy darkness of the tunnel. Jayson was only able to shine a beam on the ground and follow it, making sure not to trip.

"Anyone afraid of the dark?" Richard asked as they walked. "I suppose that if you were, it would be too late for that to matter."

No one responded.

After about ten minutes of walking, they came upon a grouping of old ground vehicles that looked to have been abandoned long ago. One car was smashed into the wall, but the others looked to have been pushed aside the way a toddler might push over a stack of building blocks. Some were lying on their sides, and others rested in awkward positions.

Jayson tried not to think of what might have done that.

The vehicles looked like they were military or scientific, either armored or loaded with some sort of analyzing equipment to monitor the surrounding environment.

"They look old," Bret said. He moved over to one and, after a few tries, managed to yank the door open. A frozen corpse slid out, hanging limply out of the vehicle. The arm snapped off and fell to the ground.

"Really old," Richard agreed. "Poor sods died out here all alone."

"We should check them for supplies," Jayson said. Richard gave him a funny look, but no one objected.

They moved quickly through the line of cars, finding a lot of small items inside, including flares and more powerful flashlights. They didn't find any weapons, though, and Jayson was starting to worry that they might really need them.

"What killed them?" Bret asked as they worked.

"No idea," Jayson said.

They found three more bodies in the wreckage, but none of them had wounds on them of any kind.

"Maybe some kind of chemical warfare," Tricia offered.

"Exactly right," a voice called from deeper down the tunnel.

Jayson turned and shone the flashlight, falling into a fighting stance. Standing a little ways farther down the tunnel from them was

156

Alexander Robertson. He was leaning on his cane and wearing an enormous winter coat that covered half of his face. He looked especially old in the tunnel.

"How long have you been standing there?" Richard asked.

"Long enough," Alexander replied, tapping his cane on the ground. "I'm glad you found the place."

"It wasn't exactly hard to find," Bret replied. "This place is huge."

"No," Alexander said. "It is difficult to miss. But, I'm pleased nevertheless."

"What are we doing here?" Jayson asked. "You said we were supposed to clear this place out, but you still haven't told us what is here."

Alexander was silent for a long minute. "Nor should I, because it violates the terms of the wager. But, since I'm not a gambling man, I am here to fill you in partly on what you will face. Do you know what the Fists of the First Citizen are?"

"So this place is related to them?" Richard said.

"Soldiers," Jayson replied, ignoring him. "The ones who were trained here before the rebellion began."

Alexander nodded. "Yes, before Darius began his crusade against the Republic. What else have you heard about the Fists?"

"That they were genetically modified," Richard said. "And that they are eight feet tall, have backup organs, and shoot lasers out of their asses."

"It's true," Alexander said. "Except the last."

"Genetic engineering is illegal," Jayson said.

"Yes, it is," Alexander agreed. "And has been since the founding of the Republic. Nevertheless, this facility was where the Fists were designed. It was never simple engineering either. These are extremes well beyond what human genetic material should be capable of. They were modified with the extreme ranges of all human traits to be superior to everyone who came before."

"What happened to this place?"

"It was attacked by a group of militants who sought to stop the genetic engineering. Gas attacks and wholesale slaughter. No one survived, militant or otherwise. Everyone was murdered and left for dead, but the Fists program was not closed, but rather moved to the Core worlds where it could be better protected."

"I knew it," Richard mumbled quietly.

"What can we expect to find inside?"

"Many creatures," Alexander said. "But also many resources and weapons. Scavengers have come through in the past, but few make it out alive."

"So, this is a test? We do this and then our training is complete?"

"*If* you survive this test, then the four of you will be sent to Sector Two. You will be responsible for creating dissent and leveraging terror against the Republic. Everything hinges on your successful completion of this task."

"Why Sector Two?"

"The Union doesn't have the resources or manpower to challenge the Republic directly, and thus we need to leverage their vast resources against them."

"Force them to waste resources trying to deal with us?" Jayson said.

Alexander nodded. "Yes."

"And what happens if they catch us?"

Alexander didn't reply this time. Jayson understood what his silence meant.

"I see," Jayson said.

"What else came through here," Tricia interrupted suddenly, still studying the ground vehicles. "No animals we've seen could do something like this."

"No, they couldn't," Alexander agreed.

"Something else came through this tunnel," she said. "There was an attack, but there are no signs of explosions, so what moved these cars? Something large must have come through here."

Alexander smiled, and tapped his cane on the ground. "Indeed something did," he said. "You'll have to clear everything out."

"You keep saying that we are supposed to clear this place out," Richard said. "Is it going to be dangerous?"

"Quite," Alexander said. "Darius intends to reopen the facility and recover the research and supplies. That is all I can tell you, and I must be off before Alyssa realizes anything is amiss."

"What sort of creatures are in there?" Jayson asked as he left. "The worst of it. Is it something we've seen before?"

"No," Alexander said. "You haven't seen anything like this before. We know very little about them, except that they are large. We call them Wyrms. They can crush a steel crate in their teeth."

"How are we supposed to kill them?" Jayson asked.

"Very carefully," Alexander replied.

"Why not just use an army?" Bret asked.

"We will, should you fail. But if you fail, it means you are dead, so I would recommend *not* failing."

"How many are there?"

"More than one," Alexander replied. "I think. It is impossible to tell. There are other things here as well that you will need to deal with. I wish I could be more specific, but I personally know very little about them. No one I have sent to deal with them made it back."

"That's reassuring," Richard said.

"In any case, this is where I leave you. Once you are finished, fire a flare into the sky and we will come to retrieve you."

"What about weapons?" Jayson asked.

Alexander shrugged. "Nothing outside is permitted during this test."

"You're kidding?"

"You'll think of something. As I said, this was a military facility where a war took place. There should be plenty of dangerous items for you to use."

Jayson thought to reply, but Alexander didn't give him the chance. He tapped his cane on the ground three times, the sound echoing, and smiled at them.

"I wish you all the best of luck," he said and then strode back the way they had come. He disappeared from their light farther up the tunnel, heading back toward the surface behind them.

They all stood for a long moment, watching him disappear.

2

"Well, crap," Richard said. "This is going to suck. When they said we were clearing this place out, I thought they meant we would be packing up and moving boxes."

"We need to have a plan," Jayson replied, shaking his head at Richard.

"Our plan needs to be to gather up whatever weapons and equipment we can find," Tricia said. "We should get moving. Our flashlights won't last forever, and we should find somewhere with better light while it is still daytime up above."

"We need to locate items we can use to defend ourselves," Bret said.

"We know this place used to have weapons, which means they must have an armory," Jayson said.

"Definitely," Bret replied. "On a planet like this, they would have needed a lot of them, and they would have kept them near their vehicles."

"Why do you think Darius wants this facility?" Richard asked. "Genetic engineering? Do you think he's going to start the program back up and build Fists of his own? If he did, I bet that would really piss the Republic off and get this war underway."

"No idea," Jayson said.

"And I don't care," Bret added. "I'm with Tricia. The sooner I have a gun in my hand, the better I'll feel."

"I don't think a gun will do much against the creatures he was describing," Richard said.

"It'll do a hell of a lot more than my fist," Bret replied. "Let's split up and search out some weapons and then group back up to start hunting."

Jayson didn't like the idea of splitting up, but he decided not to object. So far, they hadn't come across any threats, and splitting up would make it easier to find and recover equipment.

They moved forward down the tunnel until they found a four way intersection splitting away from their ramp.

"What do you guys think?"

"Impossible to tell," Bret said. "Just a crapshoot at this point."

"We'll head east," Tricia said, pointing down one of the tunnels. "You guys go the opposite direction. Meet back here in an hour whether you find something or not."

"Got it," Jayson said. The two groups split apart and headed down their respective tunnels.

Jayson stepped lightly, on his guard now that Alexander had warned them of danger. He crept along with Bret, shining his flashlight down the tunnel in front of them.

Neither man spoke as they moved through the dome. He could feel the weight of the hulking structure over his head. There were overhead lights every few meters, but without any power, they served

160

no purpose. The darkness was oppressive around them, and the air tasted stale this far underground.

After about twenty minutes of walking, they reached an enormous underground garage. It was filled with old vehicles that were abandoned and covered in a layer of permafrost. Industrial elevators dotted the floor at different points.

Throughout the area in various locations, they saw paths carved through the vehicles where cars had been haphazardly knocked out of the way. It was almost like following a deer trail through the forest, and it seemed like these trails were well used.

"Holy hell," Bret mumbled. "That thing must be huge."

"Or a lot of them," Jayson agreed.

"Do you think they stick around or just come here once in a while?"

"Impossible to tell. My guess is, though, that whatever they are, they have taken up residence here."

They spoke quietly, but their voices seemed to carry forever in the vast, empty chamber. It was eerie with everything so quiet yet designed for near constant use. The light from their flashlights couldn't even touch the walls of the underground facility as they moved closer to the center of the parking garage.

"I hate this place," Jayson muttered.

"Me too," Bret said. "It feels like something is watching us."

"Yeah."

"He called them Wyrms," Bret said. "Like dragons. You don't think..."

"Dragons aren't real."

"I know, but...there are a lot of crazy things on this planet."

"More likely it is giant snakes."

Bret was silent for a long moment. "I don't know if that is any better."

They walked in silence for another few minutes, looking around at the equipment and vehicles for anything they might be able to use. Most of the vehicles looked scientific in nature and held little of value in dealing with the creatures in this place.

The farther they went, the less confident he was that they would find an armory. Most likely it wasn't on this level, but he didn't see any easy access points to one of the levels above. They didn't have any stairs, only elevators: they clearly never expected for the power to go out.

"What's that?" Bret asked.

Jayson shone his flashlight over, adding his light to Bret's and amplifying it on a truck. It was a large off-road behemoth, military grade and covered in metallic plates. It had smashed into one of the pillars a long time ago and looked out of place.

They moved over to examine it more closely and saw that there was a pair of dead bodies inside. The icy weather had preserved them and it looked as though both had died in the crash.

"It is always cold up here," Bret said, glancing in the front window and moving around the truck. "Never thaws out. I wonder if they picked a cold climate to make it easier to preserve the things they were testing on."

"Heating must have been a bitch."

Bret shrugged. "But if something goes wrong, everything gets cold, not hot. Helps with preservation."

Inside they saw various items in disarray: a medical supply kit that had been smashed, radio and sensor equipment that was broken into pieces, and more unidentifiable wreckage.

Jayson moved around the truck and looked for a way in. The doors were locked and the windows looked to be solid, but the driver's side window had been cracked in the crash. He found a nearby chunk of the broken pillar and used it to smash open the window.

The sound echoed through the place, causing him to wince by how loud it sounded in the silence.

"Could you be any louder?" Bret asked.

Jayson ignored him. He searched through the truck, checking under the seats and in any crevice. The two dead people, both men, were unarmed and had very few things in their pockets. It looked like they had barely had time to prepare before jumping into the car and trying to drive off.

They didn't make it too far.

He got lucky when he opened the glove compartment and found a loaded pistol tucked inside, along with a lot of paperwork. It looked like a small-caliber gun, but it was certainly better than nothing.

"Thank the Ministry for small favors," he mumbled, climbing back out of the vehicle. He unlocked the doors and started moving around toward the other side of the truck, planning to check the back for anything else.

"What?" Bret asked. "Did you find something?"

Jayson turned toward him and started to answer, but the words caught in his throat. Behind Bret, maybe fifteen meters away, a giant slithering creature was gliding across the floor toward them.

It moved silently across the ice, barely making any noise at all, and was completely white and covered in thin and sparse hairs. It appeared to be about three meters long and had a giant gaping maw on the front; that maw was open as it slid toward Bret, showing lines of jagged teeth that were each the size of a short knife blade and very sharp.

"Look out," Jayson shouted, raising the pistol.

Bret ducked and jumped to the side, clearing his line of sight. Jayson took aim and squeezed the trigger.

The bullet smashed into the side of the worm, slowing it, but it wasn't enough to stop it. Jayson fired off two more rounds, placing both right into the maw of the creature, snapping teeth on the way in. The bullets ripped through the body, tearing holes through its soft skin.

It slid forward a few more meters, shuddered and let out a sharp squealing sound, and then stopped moving. It slumped to the side, oozing some sort of liquid out of its maw that sizzled when it touched the ice.

3

Jayson stared at it, panting and with adrenaline still coursing through his body. He took a few steps closer to the creature, holding the gun ready and looking around them.

He couldn't believe how quiet the creature had been moving toward them, and he was worried that another one might be sneaking up on them in the darkness. He checked with his flashlight, looking in all directions, but he couldn't see anything.

The only sound in the chamber was the breathing of the two men and the sizzling sound coming from the dead body. Something was burning the ice and seemed to be very hot as it spilled out of the creature's body.

"Damn," he said.

"Is it dead?"

"I think so."

"Is that it? Is that what Alexander warned us about?"

"I don't know."

"That thing was so quiet."

"I know. Do you see any more of them?"

Bret shook his head. "No. Just the one."

"Stay ready," Jayson said. "No telling what else might be out here."

"They look like burrowing creatures. Probably live underground."

"Most likely," Jayson said, barely paying attention. He was too busy looking out for more of them. He took a few more steps toward the dead body, hoping to examine it and find out what that sizzling noise was.

"Yeah. I mean, that wasn't actually as bad as I imagined. I was expecting something a lot worse. But if that's all there is, then this shouldn't be too bad at all—"

There was a deep rumbling sound and the ground started to shake. Jayson stepped back toward the broken truck, dancing to keep his footing on the slippery ice.

Suddenly there was a massive blasting sound on the far side of the chamber, rocking the ground as though they were at the epicenter of an earthquake. He heard the ground get ripped apart, and sections of it went flying into the ceiling and walls.

It happened about two-hundred meters away from them, but some smaller pieces still thudded into the area around them.

He ducked behind the truck, waiting for the barrage to end, and then stepped out. The ground stopped shaking, but he heard a large thudding sound as something landed on the floor of the chamber some distance away from them.

That was followed by a high-pitched squealing sound, similar to what came from the small Wyrm but significantly louder.

"What the hell was that?" Bret asked, breathless.

They heard a scraping sound as something started moving toward them. They heard vehicles being knocked out of the way as something huge slid across the chamber. Jayson felt his hands start trembling as his mind tried to picture what such a creature might look like.

"I think this was what Alexander was talking about..." Jayson muttered, backpedaling toward the entrance of the chamber.

Bret nodded at him, eyes wide.

"Run!"

Chapter 17
Sector 1 – Axis
Abdullah Al Hakir

1

The gun strapped to Abdullah's hip felt like it weighed at least a thousand pounds.

Now that he was here, standing in the same room where he'd been raised to First Officer two years earlier, the true weight of what was happening had started to settle in. It was no longer a "what if" question about how to handle the trial but had become completely real. His hands felt clammy, and he was sick to his stomach.

He'd thought he understood the weight of his decision while he debated with himself and Eddie in his chambers, but this was something different entirely. The idea that he would have to use the weapon to take a man's life...it was something he was struggling to come to terms with.

He'd already told the Captain what he intended to do and that he planned to execute Gregory Tillman for the crime of rape. However, that was before he'd come into the room and been surrounded by the other officers of *Denigen's Fist*. He knew that this proceeding was being broadcast to the entire ship, and likely beyond, which meant everyone would be watching his next moves.

Maybe it would be better if he walked his decision back? He still had time to change his mind and spare the Ensign for his crimes. After all, the only three people who knew of his decision were himself,

Eddie, and Captain Grove. Maybe a better alternative to death would be to forgive the man and give him a second chance.

He would lose the Captain's respect, but the alternative was executing a criminal in front of thousands of people. He saw the accused soldier standing on the far side of the room, covered in a sheen of sweat, an expression of terror on his face. Two guards flanked him, standing ready in case he tried to escape.

He wasn't just a name on a piece of paper anymore. He was a young man—Gods, so young—with dreams and ambitions and aspirations. He didn't look like a terrible person and, in fact, seemed more like a child than anything else.

That didn't excuse what he had done, but how could Abdullah repay one horrible act with another?

Gregory didn't know how this day would turn out; he had no idea if his First Officer would spare him or execute him, or something in between. The only thing Gregory was certain of right now was that his fate was in the hands of another man.

Abdullah's hands.

Jamir Paskin walked to the podium in front of the officers, a blank expression on his face and right hand resting comfortably on his ample stomach. He looked dignified in his *Fist* uniform despite the fact that he wasn't a soldier.

Abdullah wished he could look that dignified. Or at least as dignified as the other Officers in the room. He knew they were all judging him and doubtless they were finding him lacking in every facet that mattered. Never before had he felt more like an imposter.

Jamir waved for the guards to bring Gregory Tillman in front of the crowd. A few people murmured now that things were underway, and Abdullah felt sick to his stomach.

The guards half dragged and half carried the soldier over, holding his arms to keep him on his feet. Gregory's face was covered in a sheen of sweat, and the fear and disorientation was evident in his expression.

No, it wasn't all sweat, Abdullah realized he was also crying.

"Gregory Tillman," Jamir Paskin began, addressing both the soldier and the crowd. "You stand accused of the crime of rape against Ensign Victoria Bloom. How do you plead?"

The man mumbled something.

"Speak up and enter your plea before God and man."

"Not guilty," Gregory said, his voice barely audible.

"It shall be noted that the accused has entered a not guilty plea. However, the evidence in this case has been weighed and the decision will be presented forthwith..."

Jamir droned on, listing off the evidence against the soldier. It included the rape kit that had been gathered after the incident as well as a lot of character references and witnesses who had given testimony. No witnesses were called, and that was at Abdullah's request. He felt like the dog and pony show was elaborate enough with bringing a crying woman to the stand to explain what happened to her.

He somewhat regretted that decision now; seeing Victoria tell her story might help reinforce his confidence in the decision he had made. After all, she was the victim, not Gregory.

She hadn't been brought into the trial today, but he imagined she was watching the events take place from her quarters or maybe in the mess hall surrounded by her friends. What would she want him to do? Would she want Gregory to die?

"You okay?" Eddie whispered beside him.

Abdullah didn't look at his friend, but he did nod slightly. He had no idea if he was really okay or not, but telling Eddie about the thoughts going through his head wouldn't help anyone. He was grateful that Eddie was here with him today; he knew exactly where his friend stood on the issue and that made it a little easier to deal with. He knew that Eddie wouldn't judge him for what he was about to do.

He wasn't so sure, however, that he wouldn't judge himself.

He'd never actually killed anyone before. Decisions he made had resulted in people dying, but he was never the one to actually pull the trigger. There was always a layer of separation, but now he was trying to come to terms with the idea that he was about to actually end someone's life. He was a soldier, sure, and he had seen a lot of death...but he'd never explicitly caused it before.

"I'm all right," he lied, hoping to appease his friend.

"This is kind of crazy," Eddie said. "Are you really going to go through with it?"

"Yes. The crime needs to be dealt with harshly so that everyone understands that their actions have consequences."

"That sounds like the Captain talking."

"You supported this decision."

"It's what I would do," Eddie agreed. "But…"

"But, what?"

Eddie was silent for a long moment.

"Do you want me to do it?" Eddie asked finally. "Officers almost never carry out the actual execution after sentencing. You can just give your decree about what's going to happen, and I'll take care of it."

Abdullah let out a sigh, feeling an overwhelming feeling of love for his dear friend, but he knew he couldn't accept the offer.

'Thank you, but no," he said. "I'm the one that decided to take this man's life. What kind of leader would I be if I was too much of a coward to do it myself?"

"Good," Eddie replied, letting out a breath of air. "I'm glad you said that. I'm not sure I could have actually done it."

Abdullah fell silent, half listening to Jamir as he wrapped up delivering the information about the crime. The fat man didn't say anything about the punishment for such a crime because technically none had been decided yet.

There is still time, he knew. Time to change my mind and pardon Gregory.

But he knew he couldn't do that. Gregory had made a terrible mistake and clearly regretted his actions, yet what he'd done was unforgivable. He had harmed a young woman and needed to pay for that crime because Victoria Bloom would need to live with that her entire life.

And yet, he wondered, what life would Gregory have after he took it from him?

"First Officer Abdullah Al Hakir," Jamir said, ripping Abdullah out of his thoughts.

He blinked, realizing that the entire room was staring at him.

No doubt this wasn't the first time he'd been addressed. Many of the officers had amused expressions on their faces. Captain Grove was frowning at him. Jamir, on the other hand, seemed perfectly patient and content to wait as long as it took for Abdullah to gather his thoughts.

He cleared his throat.

"Yes?"

"Would you like to commence with the sentencing?"

Abdullah rubbed his sweaty hands on his pants. "Yes, of course."

"You've got this," he heard Eddie whisper beside him. He didn't spare a glance at his friend, but having his support meant the world to him.

He stepped out of the line of gathered officers and approached the condemned man. As he walked, he drew his pistol, feeling the weight in his hand as he hefted the weapon. He felt his hand shaking and prayed that the cameras broadcasting his image didn't catch it.

He took a deep and steadying breath, stopped behind the soldier, and said, "Gregory Tillman, you stand charged with this crime, and you have been found guilty."

He stood behind the man, watching him squirm as he heard the verdict brought down.

"No...no please..." Gregory begged, trying to pull loose and turn around to face Abdullah. "Please...you have to understand..."

The guards held him in an iron grip, refusing to let go.

Abdullah raised his gun and aimed it at the back of the man's head. The entire moment felt surreal, like he was standing outside his own body and watching it happen. He could hardly believe that this was him standing here about to execute one of his soldiers.

"Do you have anything to say for yourself?"

"Please...she was willing," Gregory pleaded. "She asked me to stop, and I should have stopped, but when we started, she was willing."

"The sentence for this crime is..."

He trailed off, feeling the words catch in his throat. Time seemed to slow down, and he could see the sweat on the back of the man's neck. He could see the way his arms twitched as he tried to jerk free.

Gregory was a young man, alive and vibrant, a living creature created by God. He was a criminal, but he was also *alive*. Abdullah had been taught from a young age by his parents that all lives were sacred and that no life should be taken when there was any alternative.

All lives were sacred, even those of a criminal.

If that was true, how could Abdullah kill this man?

The Captain wouldn't have hesitated to pull the trigger and put a bullet in Gregory's brain. She would throw him out of the ship's airlock to drift through space without a moment's hesitation and forget about him the second he was out of her line of sight.

But he wasn't the Captain.

He lowered the gun.

"Your sentence for this crime is seven years in the brig followed by a dishonorable discharge. You will be confined to a cell until the allotted time has passed without any chance of early parole."

He took a step back, breathing easier than he had in days, and holstered his weapon.

"Take him away," he ordered to the guards holding Gregory.

They dragged Gregory, who was no longer struggling, to the door and out into the hallway. He paused at the door and glanced back, a look of relief on his face.

Then he was gone, carried away to his cell.

Abdullah glanced around and saw that the entire room of officers was staring at him, many with confused expressions on their faces. Mouths were hanging open in shock, and some even looked afraid. They hadn't known explicitly what was going to happen today, but they knew what was supposed to happen.

This wasn't it.

They'd been fully expecting, like he had, to have an execution here today, and none of them seemed to know what exactly had happened.

Abdullah met Jamir's eyes. The pudgy man had a curious expression on his face, but he also looked pleased. He nodded at Abdullah, tilting his head toward the door, suggesting that maybe it was time he left.

He took the cue and walked out, not looking back. He didn't stop walking until he was back in his own chambers, and then he allowed himself to admit how afraid he was. He knew in his heart that he had made the right decision for himself. When he really thought about it, there was no way he could have gone through with executing the soldier.

Every life was sacred.

But he also knew that he'd screwed everything up with his position aboard the ship. This had been a test by the Captain, he knew.

And he had failed.

Chapter 18
Sector 4 – Alderson
Jayson Coley

1

Jayson and Bret sprinted back through the cavernous garage toward the entrance where they had first come in. They had a head start against the monster chasing them, but he could feel it closing the distance.

He glanced over his shoulder and saw an enormous creature, at least forty meters long and ten meters high, bursting out of the floor of the garage. Its screech filled the entire room, echoing off of the walls.

It landed with a thud and came after them, gliding across the ground like a huge snake. It was white and covered in scales, a larger version of the one they had killed.

"I think you killed one of its kids," Bret shouted.

"I realized that."

"What do we do now?"

Jayson ignored him and kept running. He knew the pistol he was carrying was still loaded, but he also knew it wouldn't do them a lot of good against something that huge. The bullets would barely even hurt it.

They needed something bigger.

The ground shook as the creature slid after them, and it moved with speed and grace despite its size. They reached the divide in the tunnel.

"This way," Jayson shouted, taking the tunnel where Richard and Tricia had gone earlier.

He doubted they would be able to do anything to help, but strength in numbers seemed like a good idea right about now. With any luck, they would find an armory and some larger weapons they might use against the Wyrm.

It was only about thirty meters behind them now and closing fast, but the tunnel was narrowing and the creature was having a harder time sliding through. This tunnel went up and into the facility, entering into another section that looked entirely different.

The tunnel emptied into an expansive courtyard that was completely enclosed by the dome above. It was full of dead trees and flowers that were covered in a layer of permafrost and looked like it hadn't been occupied in centuries.

Sunlight filtered in from the dome up above through the glass panels, showing them a gruesome sight: some thirty bodies were stacked in the corner of the room, riddled with bullet holes and forgotten.

"Where?" Bret shouted.

Jayson glanced around and saw two pairs of boot prints leading off to the left. These looked newer, fresh, and doubtless belonged to their companions.

The creature screeched behind them, close now. Jayson glanced back and saw jagged lines of teeth only a few meters away. These teeth were huge, each bigger than his legs, and he could feel intense heat radiating from the creature.

"This way," he said, turning and sprinting after the footprints. They led to an entrance into the facility-proper, a massive structure built up against the side of the dome along the northern side.

The entrance was huge and connected to a lot of other passageways. Long corridors led into separate chambers and offices.

This section of the building had a high ceiling, and only a small amount of light from the roof made it into here. Jayson knew that the creature would have no trouble following them, which meant they needed to find a tighter passageway to get away from it.

"Hurry!" Bret said, pointing ahead toward one of the hallways. "It can't fit there!"

They sprinted, ground shaking, and stumbled into the hallway a few steps ahead of the creature. It tried to follow but got stuck a few meters into the corridor, completely blocking the exit. The light disappeared, blocked by the creature's body, but they still had their flashlights.

Bret stopped a few meters farther in and turned to look at the Wyrm, panting.

"It can't fit in here," he said, wiping off his brow. "Good."

The maw opened and the creature made a screeching sound, straining to push closer to them. It tried to contract its body, but it was simply too big to force its way through.

"We're safe," Bret said. "Thank God."

Jayson glanced at him just as the creature pulled back out of the hallway. He saw two tubes protrude from the sides of its mouth, just under the teeth. It opened the mouth wider, aiming those tubes at them.

"Uh oh," he said, turning and grabbing Bret.

"What?"

Jayson didn't reply except to drag Bret farther down the hall and away from the creature. A few seconds later, he heard a splashing sound behind them, followed by a burning hiss.

When he looked back, he saw the hallway walls melting. The creature was spraying something—maybe acid—onto them, and where the liquid touched, it burned right through it.

After a few seconds, the creature started moving again, tearing through the softened section of wall and sliding forward to them.

When Jayson turned and looked at his friend, he saw that Bret was pale and terrified.

"Oh," Bret said, turning and running.

Jayson followed, and they raced farther down the hall to stay ahead of the creature. He heard it spraying more, and he wondered how much of that fluid it could store up before it would need to make more. With luck, it would run out soon and need to rest before trying to pursue them.

2

They rushed down the corridor, passing by old offices. Many of the doors were broken open and there were halls in the walls the farther in they went. It looked like a large number of smaller creatures had traveled through here and created their own passageways.

They heard the enormous monster screeching behind them, trying to push through the walls and give chase. It made the entire structure shake, but the sounds diminished the farther into the facility they went.

They turned down a series of corridors before finally finding their way into an old laboratory. Broken equipment and glass beakers were covered in a layer of frost. There were at least thirty workstations in the room, and they were covered in broken old equipment. It looked like much of it had been destroyed years ago, but some of it seemed like it might still work after being thawed out.

Off to the right was an empty chamber with a ring painted in the center of the floor with different colored wedges in the center.

"What is that?"

"Probably for experimenting," Jayson replied. "Help me check around. We need weapons."

They tore through the room, looking for anything they might use against the creature chasing them. He didn't think they would get lucky enough to find a gun, but right now, he would take anything.

He found an old cabinet loaded with supplies. There were some in there he could use to create a bomb, he knew, but right now everything was either frozen or the bottles would need to be thawed out before he could risk using them.

"Here," Bret called behind him.

He turned and saw Bret opening an emergency box with an axe inside. However, when it swung open, he saw that the box was empty.

"Probably Richard and Tricia," Jayson said. It was a good sign, meaning they were probably still on the trail of their friends.

"I don't think there's anything else we can use."

"Probably not. Come on, we need to keep moving."

They wove around the tables, feeling the ground shake as the creature tore its way toward them. Luckily, it didn't seem to be able to burrow very fast through the heavier materials of the facility.

"How the hell do we kill that thing?" Bret asked.

"No clue."

"Where did Richard and Tricia go?"

Jayson only shook his head in response, looking around for an exit to the lab. There was a door leading farther into the facility as well as a staircase leading up. He wished he had a map of the layout so he knew which direction might be best.

"We need to figure out how we can hurt it," Bret said.

"I know."

"Which way?"

Jayson hesitated, wondering which way Richard and Tricia might have gone, and then gestured toward the stairs. "Up."

They rushed up the stairs, heading into another section of laboratories and testing areas. This one was full of half-finished experiments and larger equipment designed to filter out DNA and chemicals. There were also several bodies in here.

"Look out!" Bret shouted, pointing to the right side of the room.

Jayson glanced over and started to raise his pistol. Another of the smaller Wyrms was in the corner of the room. However, on closer inspection, he realized that it wasn't moving and its lower half was covered in a thick brown ichor.

Still holding the pistol ready, he moved across the floor toward it. Once he got closer, he realized it was dead: deep wounds riddled its side.

"Looks like Tricia got the better of this one."

"They have to be close."

Jayson moved over to the creature, grabbing a large pair of tongs from one of the work stations. He used it to push open the creature's mouth.

"See if you can find a knife," he said.

Bret scurried around for a second and then came over to Jayson carrying what looked like a large pocketknife. He flicked open the blade, held open the mouth, and started digging around where the protruding section had been in the larger Wyrm.

"What are you looking for?"

"To see if they can spit acidic bile, too."

"And?"

Jayson shook his head, letting the mouth close once more. "Doesn't look like it. That must be something they develop later in life."

"Reassuring," Bret said. "Do you hear it anymore?"

He stepped back and listened. The complex was quiet, and he couldn't hear the larger creature tearing through the walls anymore.

"No. I don't hear it."

"Do you think it gave up? Maybe we lost it."

"I don't know, but I doubt it. It might be able to track us."

"I hope not," Bret said.

"Me too," Jayson said. "But we need to expect the worst. It probably never comes up here, but I think we might have given it a reason to."

Jayson felt adrenaline coursing through his veins and knew he would crash before too long.

"We need to get moving and find the others before it finds us."

They moved out the laboratories and into living quarters. The floor in this section of the complex was carpeted, though everything was covered in a layer of frost. Numbered doors led out of the main hallway into small apartments, no bigger than one bedroom apiece.

Many of them had been broken into, and recently. It looked like Tricia and Richard were using their axe as a key and searching door to door. Jayson thought to call ahead and see if they were nearby, but he was worried that there might be other things in the area.

Bodies littered this section in various states of decomposition, many of them covered in frost or snow. More light came in through the ceiling, but they were still using their flashlights to see things clearly.

It looked like the militants had made it to this area first; many of the scientists here had been executed, some in the hallway and others in their apartments. They looked wholly unprepared to defend themselves.

"There have to be hundreds," Jayson said, moving down the hallway in awe. "Thousands maybe."

"All dead," Bret agreed. "Scientists and biologists. These weren't soldiers. They didn't deserve this."

"They were dealing with genetic engineering. It's illegal."

"Not all of them, and even then they didn't deserve this."

Jayson didn't argue, not really having a good answer. He personally felt that genetic engineering was wrong, but he couldn't have given a good explanation of why. There was something unnatural about it that raised the hairs on his arms.

Still, murdering people in cold blood...

They continued walking down the hallway, turning a corner and moving deeper into the living quarters. They traveled for another couple of minutes before they started to hear some weird noises from up ahead.

"What is that?"

"I don't know," Jayson said. "It sounds like...is that someone singing?"

They glanced at each other, and both said, "Richard."

As they grew closer, they started to relax, realizing it was their friend belting out the lyrics of a song. They found him and Tricia rummaging in one of the side rooms. Tricia was carrying the axe and watching the hallway, and Richard was haphazardly tossing things.

Tricia nodded at them as they approached, acting as though nothing was amiss.

"What are you guys doing?" Jayson asked.

Richard stopped singing and turned toward them. He picked a rifle up off the bed, but relaxed when he saw it was them.

"Searching," Richard said.

"And singing?"

"Passes the time."

Jayson glanced at Tricia, who was frowning. "I couldn't get him to stop."

"You guys didn't hear that back there?"

"Hear what?"

Jayson and Bret exchanged a glance. "We need to find weapons."

"We found some," Richard said. "One of the militants was swarmed by scientists and taken down, and we found a rifle and pistol."

Jayson looked skeptically at the gun Tricia was holding.

"Bigger ones."

3

"What do you mean? We found one in those rooms a while back, and they aren't too bad."

"Those are the babies," Jayson explained.

Richard hesitated. "Scale?"

"Maybe one-twentieth full size."

"You saw one?"

He nodded. "Pretty sure we pissed it off."

178

"Why'd you do that?"

Jayson ignored him. "We're going to need something huge to get rid of it."

"How huge?"

"A cannon, maybe."

"It can't get in here," Tricia interrupted, looking at the hallway behind them. "If it's as big as you say, then it won't be able to fit down the hallway."

"It can burrow," Jayson explained. "It shoots out jets of acid that can burn through the walls."

Richard blanched. "No kidding?"

"I wish I was," Jayson said.

"Only the one?" Tricia asked.

Jayson nodded. "That, and a handful of small ones, probably."

"We saw a vehicle parked outside," Tricia said, "when we were first checking these rooms out. It looks to have been abandoned by the militants outside the dome when they came in, but it's still in good shape. It's laying on its side, but it looks to have a heavy gun mounted on it."

"Show it to us," Jayson said.

"All right, we saw it back this way—"

Just then, there was an enormous crashing sound in the hallway behind them. Jayson rushed past Tricia and saw the Wyrm burrowing through the floor from the level below. The screeching sound filled the hallway, hurting his ears, and he winced.

"Guess that means it can track us," he mumbled.

He glanced back and saw terrified expressions on the faces of Tricia and Richard.

"What the hell...?" Richard muttered.

"Where is the vehicle?" Jayson asked. "We need to get to it."

"Back that way," Tricia said, pointing past the Wyrm. It made a screeching sound as it pulled up to their level, and Jayson saw the acid spitters protruding from its maw.

"Get back," he said, pulling them farther into the room.

He heard a spraying sound and saw the acid hitting the floor and walls in the hallway outside the room. It ate everything it touched, melting the floor in front of their eyes.

"What do we do?" Richard asked.

Tricia picked up the rifle and leaned into the hallway, firing a few rounds back at the Wyrm. She ducked back as another spray of acid landed around her.

"Anything?"

"I hit it," she said. "But I don't think it did much damage."

"I told you, we need something bigger. Do you think we can get to the vehicle?" Jayson asked.

"If we can get outside the dome," Tricia said. "But I didn't see any exits."

"What about this stuff?" Richard asked, gesturing his arm toward the acid.

The ground started shaking as the Wyrm dragged itself up into the hallway, tearing the entire structure apart around it. The walls crumpled and the floor shook under its weight. They were all knocked off balance as it moved slowly toward them, letting out another shriek.

4

"We need to go down," Jayson said. The acid was eating through the floor, creating small holes, but not fast enough. He couldn't risk getting any on his skin and clothes. He glanced back in the scientists' room and saw a large dresser resting along one wall.

"Help me," he said to Richard, grabbing one side of it and trying to get a good grip.

"What are we doing with it?"

Richard grabbed the other side, lifting it up. Jayson guided him, and they carried it to the doorway.

"Throwing it. When I say now, push it out as far as you can and let it fall onto the floor. Got it?"

"Got it."

Jayson lined it up, getting his body out of the way as much as possible. He swung the dresser to gain some momentum and then shouted, "Now!"

Richard shoved the dresser out as Jayson side-stepped out of the way. It felt into the hallway and smashed into the floor. It was weakened by the acid, and the dresser crashed through, falling down to the level below with an enormous thudding sound as it broke apart. The next level was about ten meters below them.

"Let's go."

Jayson didn't waste any time before jumping down after it. He was careful to land on the broken wood and not to touch any of the side walls or flooring with his clothing or skin. He landed lightly on the floor and dove into a roll, coming to his feet a few meters away.

The rest jumped down after him, Tricia and Bret landing gracefully and Richard hitting with a resounding thud, falling onto his side a short distance away.

"Ah!" he shouted, staggering to his feet and ripping his coat off. He'd brushed it against something and Jayson could see it sizzling where the acid burned through.

"Stop messing around," Jayson admonished, surveying the area around them.

They were in a storage area full of boxes and crates that were full of frozen foodstuffs and supplies forgotten years earlier. On the far side of the room was an exit door leading out of the facility.

The problem was, it was a good hundred meters away across empty space. There was nothing to slow the Wyrm down, and it moved quite a bit faster than they did across open ground.

Off to his right he could see the bottom half of the Wyrm slithering across piles of broken and discarded boxes. It hadn't managed to lift its entire body up to the next floor and was currently trying to slide backward to the level below.

To his left he saw what looked like maintenance rooms. Huge pipes and equipment sat quietly against the walls. That was only ten or so meters away, but it wouldn't get them any closer to their objective.

He didn't have a lot of time to decide on the best course of action: They needed to get to the vehicle, but not while the Wyrm was chasing them. They needed a distraction.

"Give me the gun," he said, turning to Tricia. "Get outside and get the vehicle ready. I'll get its attention."

She handed him the rifle and nodded. She turned toward the door on the far side of the dome leading outside and started sprinting. Bret ran after her, but Richard hesitated.

"Are you going to be all right?"

"I'll be fine," he said, having no clue if that was true. "Now go."

Richard turned and rushed off, chasing after the other two.

Jayson turned toward the Wyrm, which had almost wriggled loose of the ceiling, and raised the rifle. He doubted he could do more than sting or annoy it, but at least he could keep it focused on him.

He fired, hitting it in the soft underbelly. Ichor spewed out, but it didn't burn where it touched like the acid. The creature screeched in pain and writhed around angrily. Jayson took off running back into the facility, heading for the maintenance rooms. He heard it smash into the ground, shattering boxes behind him as it gave chase, sliding across the floor.

He ducked around a pile of crates and looked for an open door he could use. There was a loading ramp up ahead, but the sliding door looked to have been sealed up years earlier. He doubted he could break it open before the creature was on him.

He turned instead toward a storage room off to his left. He glanced back before heading inside and saw that Tricia and the rest had made it out of the facility. The creature didn't seem to care about them at all and was entirely focused on him.

He fired off another round into the creature, but this one didn't seem to do as much damage. When he pulled the trigger again, though, it just clicked. He tossed the gun to the floor and ran toward the facility.

Jayson rushed into the room and saw rows and rows of pods. They looked like they were designed to hold humans, but they were quite a bit bigger than he would have thought necessary. He could have fit three of himself in each one and still had room to spare.

They had glass openings on the top where the face would be where someone could look inside. As he ran down one of the rows toward the far side of the room, he glanced in those windows: most of them were empty, but every once in a while he saw a child's face in them.

They all looked to be dead, or maybe they were only incubating. He doubted any of them had survived considering the power in the facility was out.

They all looked so young and tiny in the chambers. This must be where they were engineering the soldiers, Jayson realized. The thought horrified him, realizing this was basically just a little factory full of child soldiers.

Behind him, he heard the Wyrm thud into the wall, trying to break through. It screeched, burrowing through the cement, and he saw part of its maw come through the wall.

Jayson turned and fired back at it with his pistol, landing two solid shots that didn't seem to have any effect. He turned and sprinted, heading for a maintenance hatch leading up out of the room with a ladder.

He reached the door just as the creature broke through. The hatch wasn't locked, but it was frozen. He climbed up the ladder and jarred it with his shoulder. It took him three hits—and a sore shoulder—to get it open, and he pushed his way up just as the creature slid into the room behind him.

He heard a spray of acid fly out of the creature's mouth: It hit the wall behind him, scorching it, and a little hit the side of his coat. He scurried up the ladder to the next floor into another room. It was pitch black inside, so he couldn't see anything around him.

But he could hear a hissing sound that wasn't very encouraging. There was something in the room he couldn't see, and he was fairly confident he'd just woken it up.

He quickly jerked his coat off, careful not to touch the acid with his skin, and tossed it on the floor. Being free of it gave him more mobility, but he knew it wouldn't be a good thing to go too long without it; it was too cold and frostbite would set in after only minutes if he wasn't careful.

Not that he would worry about that now. His eyes adjusted a little bit, and he scanned the new room he was in and saw that it was some sort of engineering room. Equipment dotted the walls, and the ladder led up to another landing.

In the center of the room was a pile of white snakes, probably the large Wyrm's babies. They were curled in with each other, hissing at him.

"Oh, hell no," Jayson said. "Not more of you guys."

As if in response, they started sliding across the floor at him, baring little teeth. He turned and started climbing up the rungs once more, heading higher. This was a service ladder connecting maintenance rooms, so it kept going up after the second floor, then the third, and finally up to the roof.

He heard the creature below bashing its way up through the floor beneath him in pursuit. He glanced down and saw the little snakes climbing up the ladder as well, twining their way up toward him much faster than should have been possible.

"God, I hate snakes," he said, turning back toward the exit hatch leading to the roof. The tube he was in felt tight and suffocating, and he bit back his panic to focus on the task at hand. He tested the latch.

This one was locked. He fished his gun out, leaned back and closed his eyes, and pulled the trigger.

It clicked.

"Son of a..."

He heard the hissing as the snakes came near him and tried to ignore it. He flipped the gun in his hand and started bashing the grip into the lock, trying to snap it. It was solid, but ice had weakened it, and on the fourth hit it shattered.

Sunlight poured in, and he heard the creatures hissing below. He dragged himself up into the light and rolled out onto the roof. The wind whipped at his clothing and skin, freezing his sweat in seconds.

He staggered back to his feet and rushed across the slippery dome. He ran back the way where Tricia and the rest of them were at, out beside the dome. With any luck, they'd had enough time to get the vehicle and gun working.

The dome sloped at a gentle angle near the center. It was built from alternating solar panels and glass to let light into the facility below. There was a layer of ice on it that made it slick and hard to move across. He skated across the dome, moving as fast as he could. He heard the creature bursting through the floors behind him, climbing up to the roof.

It sounded pissed.

The angle of the dome gradually grew steeper until he was forced to sit down and slide forward slowly. He could see a vehicle in the distance below as well as little figures moving around it.

They had managed to get the vehicle standing up, and it looked like Bret was messing with the controls on the gun. They were in trouble if he couldn't get it working.

"Is it working?" he shouted down.

They glanced up at him, surprised to see him on the roof.

"What are you doing up there?" Richard shouted, cupping his hands around his mouth.

"Is the damn gun working?"

"Bret's fixing it," Richard shouted up.

184

"What the hell does that mean?"

"It means we're working on it," Tricia shouted. "Where's it at?"

As if in response, the Wyrm burst through the roof behind him, sliding onto the slippery surface and screeching at him. Jayson glanced behind him and saw the creature sliding gracefully across the roof. The glass panels crunched underneath it, but they didn't give out.

He couldn't stay up here, which meant his only option was to go down. The roof was domed, but at a steep angle, and the layer of ice ran down the entire side. Once he started moving, he wouldn't be able to control his descent or his speed.

Still, he didn't have a lot of options. He looked around and saw a large sheet of metal broken off of an enormous exhaust duct. He ran over and picked it up, breaking the ice off of it. It was sturdy enough to hold him.

"This is going to suck," he mumbled, setting the sheet of metal down and sitting on top of it. He could hear the Wyrm behind him, only about thirty meters.

He curled the edges enough to hold onto and hoped they couldn't cut into his hand, and then he pushed himself forward.

5

He expected a gentle increase in acceleration once he got moving, but that wasn't what happened. The ice was slick and wet, offering no resistance at all. It felt like he was instantly flying down the side of the dome, slipping across the icy surface with almost no friction. He felt the speed building up, wind whipping across his face as he sped toward the bottom.

It was freezing without his coat, and he felt the icy air whipping his undershirt. He couldn't hear anything, but he had no doubt that the creature was still chasing him.

His fear was realized a moment later when he saw a huge blob of acid splash against the roof in front of him, burning the ice and sending up clouds of steam.

He leaned on his makeshift toboggan, sliding around the acid and continuing down the dome. He saw his three companions below, readying the gun and shouting something at him. The words were muffled, though, and there was no way to tell what they were trying to say.

He slid off the dome and onto the ground at an odd angle. The tip of his metal sled caught on the snow and tipped forward, not sliding cleanly in. It threw him like a catapult, and he hit the snow about eight meters away, bouncing into an embankment and rolling farther.

It knocked the wind out of him, and he saw stars as he tried to get his bearings. He'd never been so cold in his entire life, and he could feel his body starting to shut down.

He reoriented himself and climbed to his feet, trying to move toward his friends. He glanced behind him. It looked like the Wyrm wasn't having much luck with the roof either, sliding and bouncing its way down the surface after him. He could see it scrabbling for purchase, but it couldn't get a good enough grip to stop its momentum.

Jayson turned and worked through the snow away from the complex, putting as much separation as possible between himself and the creature. The vehicle was maybe ten meters away. Bret was done messing with it and Richard had taken up position as gunner, aiming back at the Wyrm.

"Will it shoot?" he asked, holding his chest and gasping.

Richard grinned at him. "Let's find out."

Richard pulled the trigger and the sound of gunfire filled the air. The gun laid down a heavy line of fire with high-caliber rounds, tearing into the Wyrm as it slid down the dome. Many rounds missed and ripped into the building beyond, shattering glass panels and doing untold other damage. Those rounds would do a lot of damage before stopping, he knew.

Richard continued firing for a full thirty seconds before the gun started clicking, out of rounds. But by then, he didn't need to shoot anymore. The rounds were explosive, and they ripped the Wyrm to shreds, tearing out massive chunks.

It lay on the ground, twitching with blood and gore oozing out. They watched it writhing in its death throes, making gasping noises. It took a full thirty seconds for it to finish dying.

"Easy peasy," Richard said, stepping back from the gun. He was still grinning.

"Easy for you to say," Jayson mumbled.

186

"Let's hope that was the only one," Bret said.

Richard climbed down from the gunner position. "I want one of these."

Jayson ignored them both, watching the creature die and trying to catch his breath. He was freezing and he felt miserable, but it was also exhilarating. This was by far the most dangerous position he'd ever been in, and he had to admit that he loved the thrill of it.

He staggered forward and Bret caught him, helping him toward the vehicle.

"I couldn't get the damn thing to start, but I think I can rewire it and at least get the heat on."

Jayson nodded, collapsing into the seat. Richard and Tricia piled in next to him, and Bret worked near the front, fiddling with the mechanical equipment. After a few minutes, they heard a loud banging sound from the engine, followed by a hum.

Bret climbed into the front seat and closed the door. Heat started pouring in, and it didn't take long for Jayson to start feeling his fingers and muscles once again. His body ached from the cold and getting tossed like a ragdoll.

But he also felt pretty good. The creature was dead; he'd won (sort of) and it was a great feeling. After only a few minutes, the adrenaline wore out and exhaustion crept in. Before he realized what was happening, Jayson was asleep.

6

By the time he woke up, it was nightfall, and he was alone in the vehicle. His body was aching and he felt terrible with a raging headache. It was quiet, and it took him a moment to realize that the sound of the engine was gone. He had a blanket tossed over him, but it was starting to get cold.

He pulled the blanket up higher and glanced around the vehicle, looking for any sign of where his friends might have gone. The facility looked quiet and empty, like a hulking behemoth in the snow. He could vaguely see the body of the Wyrm out in the snow, but it looked smaller now. Deflated and definitely dead.

After a few minutes of waiting, he saw a shape come out of the facility and start walking toward him. He felt around and found his pistol lying on the seat next to him. He quickly saw that he wouldn't need it, though, when he realized the form was Richard.

His friend climbed into the car, rubbing his hands together. "Super cold now," he said.

"Clearing the place out?"

"About halfway done," Richard explained. "Just wanted to come check on you. Make sure nothing ate you while you were sleeping."

"That's reassuring."

"We found about ten more of those little Wyrms so far and some ugly little baby ones. There were two nests full of them we wiped out."

"Nothing else?"

"Looks like anything else that wandered close was turned into food. We also found an armory. Fully stocked."

Jayson nodded.

"How are you feeling?" Richard asked.

"Like I just got beat up."

"You'll be fine. Tricia and Bret should be back in a couple of minutes, and we'll get the hell out of here."

They sat in the quiet car, listening to the sound of the wind whipping around the car. It was another fifteen minutes before Bret and Tricia returned, carrying supplies and weapons.

Tricia climbed into the vehicle next to Richard, and Bret dug through the supplies until he found a flare gun. He offered it to Jayson.

"Do you want to do the honors? I'm pretty sure we'd all be dead if it wasn't for you."

Jayson shrugged. "Sure."

He accepted the offered flare gun and fired off two rounds into the sky. They flew up, signaling their position, and slowly dissipated.

"Now what?" Richard asked.

"We wait," Jayson said.

Only a few minutes later, they heard enormous aerial vehicles flying in. Massive armored helicopters dropped in around them, unloading troops. Armored soldiers poured out, hundreds of them, and headed into the facility.

They completely ignored the four sitting in the Humvee. After the soldiers had finished unloading, they saw Alexander and Maven step out of one of the helicopters and start walking toward them.

188

Alexander seemed pleased when he saw that they were all alive. With Maven, however, it was impossible to tell under her breathing mask and hood. She folded her arms, watching them.

"We survived," Richard offered, breaking the silence.

"Never doubted you," Alexander said.

"What happens now?" Jayson asked.

"Now," Maven interrupted, "we bring down the Republic."

Chapter 19
Sector 6 – Eldun
Vivian Drowel

1

Vivian knew they were too late to get inside without any problems: The city was locked down tight. Vivian scouted the exterior fences around the shipyard and saw that there were guards posted at every entrance and possible weak point as well as frequent patrols.

She hadn't really expected anything different considering there was an army bearing down on Delphi, but she'd been hopeful that they might be able to easily slip inside while they were distracted. After all, the army would likely make contact on the other side of the city where it would be easier to breach.

The spaceport in particular was well defended, and she knew it would be difficult to get to her ship and slip away unnoticed. She doubted they would let her leave with their confiscated goods, and they had enough firepower to shoot her down before she made it very far.

Which meant they were trapped between an army and the gates of the city. She would need to come up with a new plan to get herself and Traq to safety.

She went back to their campsite and found Traq lying up against a tree and rubbing his legs. He was disheveled and exhausted, in need of a good bath and a few nights of restful sleep. His clothes were torn and dirty.

She doubted she looked much better right now. They hadn't packed enough goods for an extended rush like this, hoping to have time to rest and clean their supplies. She was running on empty.

But she was also reinvigorated. After the events from the previous day, she was more determined than ever to see herself and Traq to safety. She needed to find out what he was capable of and test his limits. He didn't seem to have much control over his powers, using them haphazardly in times of great stress.

He was something else entirely: she'd known that from the first day she saw him on Geid, and now she knew that it was her singular duty in life to keep him safe and find out what he would be capable of.

"How are you feeling?" she asked.

"Tired," he said. "And hungry."

"Do you want another energy bar?" she asked. They still had plenty of those high-density protein bars that the general's people had packed for them, but they had run out of most other rations during the trek.

She pulled one of the peanut butter-flavored bars out of her pack and offered it to him.

He shook his head. "No thanks," he said. "I hate those."

"Me too."

"Do we have anything else?"

"Not right now," she said.

"Okay."

"We can get better food soon," she promised. "But for now, you'll have to eat this to keep your energy up."

He sighed and then accepted the food. She grabbed one for herself as well, and they sat down to eat. She didn't disagree at all with him because they were terrible. For the first few days, they had only been a nuisance, but now she couldn't think of anything she'd rather eat less.

For a while, the only sounds were them munching on their protein bars. She could tell how tired they both were and wondered if maybe she should break into the city on her own. If she could get inside and get to the ship, maybe she could pick him up on the way out. After all, he was only a kid, and this was a lot for him to handle.

The only problem with that plan was that the longer they stayed inside the atmosphere of the planet, the more likely it was that they would be able to shoot her down. Every second mattered in a situation like this.

Worse, she would also have to find somewhere safe for him to stay while she was gone, and that ran the risk of someone stumbling upon him and either killing him or taking him captive. He could handle himself, at least a little bit, but he didn't know how to control his powers.

"Do you have a headache?" she asked.

He looked at her, confused. "No. I don't think so."

"Nothing hurts?"

"My body hurts, but my head feels fine."

She nodded, a little surprised. He didn't seem impacted by what he had done. When she was a child, using even a little bit of her mental power drained her and left her weary for hours, sometimes days. And that was when she did nothing compared to what he had done.

The effects were always worse on children than on adults, but on top of that Traq wasn't normal anyway. It was crazy to think that in everything he had done on this planet, he'd never really tested the limits of his abilities.

And yet, he hadn't complained of a headache even once, and he didn't seem any more tired than he had before he had used his gifts.

She had wondered during the last two years if maybe manifesting his powers to throw that bully so long ago on Geid had been a fluke. Maybe it was just some sort of accident of providence or maybe a one-off incident that he would never replicate.

But now she knew it wasn't. Traq was something else entirely, something she'd never even dreamt of existing before. No one had, not even the Ministry. It was exciting because she knew this was something new in the galaxy; this was something the Ministry had never faced before.

It was also terrifying. If Traq was this powerful at such a young age, what might he be capable of as he got older?

She needed to give him some sort of stress test. Push him to his breaking point and get a sense of what he was capable of, but she needed to do it in a more controlled situation away from this war and the marching armies.

She would train him effectively and teach him how to control his powers. The damage he could cause was immense, and he needed to better understand what was happening and how it was happening so that he might be able to control it.

Which meant he needed an implant. They were used to harness and control the power as much as anything, and with it she could begin teaching him techniques to regulate and focus his energy.

She had no clue how she might go about getting him such an implant, though, considering they were strictly regulated and managed by the Ministry. Argus might be willing to help, but this would be a much bigger ask than anything she'd sought before.

Still, once she explained what had happened here on Eldun, she had no doubt that Argus would be on board with her plans, if for no other reason than that he might selfishly believe he could control and use him. She would never let Argus do such a thing, but if making him believe it was a possibility got her what she wanted, she wasn't above insinuating.

But, to be honest, that was a problem for another day. Right now she had to focus on getting into the spaceport and getting off of Eldun.

2

Vivian gently kicked Traq on the side when he started snoring. He was a small child, but she couldn't believe how loudly he slept. It was like listening to a lumberjack sawing logs.

She was confident in the place she'd picked for their camp, hidden in a ravine surrounded by dense foliage, but not confident enough to let her guard down. They couldn't afford for anyone to overhear in case there were any scouts or soldiers patrolling nearby.

He coughed and sputtered but barely woke up. Groggy, he rolled over onto his side and was breathing deeply and asleep in only seconds.

She almost laughed at the absurdity of it: There was an army marching down on them only a few kilometers away to the north, and here he was fast asleep and oblivious to it all. She considered herself to be a fairly stoic person, able to keep her cool in the toughest of situations, but even her nerves were starting to act up with the intensity of it all. And yet, here he was sleeping through their precarious situation.

She'd been in a lot of fights, even to the point of full-scale battles against enemies of the Republic. She'd been a part of crushing a rebellion in Sector Seven years ago and killed her fair share of civilians and soldiers. But she had never been in the middle of a warzone alone like this, completely and wholly unprepared, and she didn't know what to expect.

She had watched their defenses and resolved herself to the reality that they wouldn't be able to sneak into the city while it was on high alert. Their defenses were solid, and they would need to wait until there was a sizable distraction before breaking in.

As soon as the battle commenced between the two armies, she was going to wake Traq, break into the spaceport, and get onto *Junker*, and then fly off world. Her hope was that the heat of the battle would be enough to distract the patrolling soldiers enough to let her get past.

But for now, it was the waiting that was getting to her. They'd already been here for several hours, and her adrenaline was wearing off. She'd scouted the advancing army earlier, and she knew they would attack sometime during the night.

Delphi knew it as well. The city was lit up with enormous searchlights and she could see soldiers walking around the fences, staring out into the woods and on edge. It was near dusk, and they knew it wouldn't be long before the shooting started.

And still Traq slept through it all.

When the attack finally started, it caught her completely off guard. It began with scattered tapping sounds in the distance, followed by shouts inside the city. All of this was followed by the war sirens. They were loud, waking up the entire city and preparing them for action.

This happened over the course of a few minutes, and then all at once the city erupted into chaos. The pattering was replaced with the roar of cannons and heavier guns, and these were much closer than the initial skirmish.

She heard people screaming and barking orders from farther in the shipyard, organizing some sort of a response to the attack, and through it all the sirens continued to blare.

She shook Traq awake, clamping a hand over his mouth to make sure he didn't cry out. He blinked up at her blearily, trying to orient himself. He looked so young and fragile, and she wondered yet again how and why she'd gotten him stuck in the middle of this warzone.

Poor life choices, she knew.

But there was no time to worry about that now. She helped him to his feet, grabbed the remainder of their meager supplies, and pointed toward the fence.

"We need to hurry. You good?"

Traq nodded and ducked low, running across the ground toward the edge of the city. Inside the fenced in spaceport they saw soldiers running around and shouting, trying to get organized. Most of them were leaving, heading to the northern side of the city where the army was attacking from. The soldiers ran around in various states of disarray, trying to put on their uniforms and carrying rifles and other supplies for the battle.

Not all were leaving to join the battle, though; some were sticking around in case another attack came to this area, but so far no one seemed to notice the two approaching from the south. Vivian hunched over and ran behind Traq, eyes peeled for any sort of threat she might have to deal with across the open field. The sirens intensified as they grew closer.

They reached the fence without anyone noticing them or calling out a warning. The fence was ten meters tall and angled outward with barbed wire. Too difficult to climb. She would have to improvise.

She reached out through her implant, touching the part of her mind that interacted with the world, and focused on the fence. It was likely electrified, which meant touching would be dangerous. She grasped the metal mentally and began unraveling it.

It was a difficult task, tapping into the molecules and separating them. If she actually stopped to think about what she was doing, separating the bonds that held the atoms together and pulling at all apart, she would have been awestruck by what was happening.

But she had learned how to do things like this at an early age, and it just sort of happened. She thought about the task at a high level, and her mind and the implant helped her actually handle the low-level task.

She pulled the fence apart in a section and lifted it out of the way, gesturing for Traq to go through. She'd worried that some sort of alarm might sound if the fence was breached, but it looked like she'd lucked out.

Traq slid in first, ducking under the broken fence and climbing onto the spaceport. Vivian moved in after him, releasing her hold on the fence and letting it hang loose. The electrical connection was still flowing through it, so it was still dangerous, but this section now had a huge gap in it.

Searchlights were sweeping the area of the shipyard between them and where *Junker* was resting, and she knew it would be nearly impossible to get across the open yard without being seen. Now, she knew, it was all or nothing in getting aboard their ship and escaping. No turning back.

3

They were committed, so waiting around wasn't an option. She grabbed Traq by the wrists and moved forward toward the enormous structure housing her ship. She timed the movement of the lights to try and weave across the yard without getting spotted. Her ship was docked in Bay Four, which was about two hundred meters away.

They moved, stopping occasionally to retime their movements or avoid a patrol. They stayed low to the ground, doing their best to stay out of sight, but it was all a matter of luck now considering they were in the open.

Her luck ran out when they were only forty meters away from Bay Four. A pair of vehicles came roaring out from behind one of the buildings up ahead of them, heading toward the battle lines to the north.

She tried to grab Traq and move out of the way before the convoy came into sight, but one of the drivers noticed her and slammed on the breaks.

The vehicle was about ten meters away from them and the driver was staring right at her. She heard shouting and one of the doors opened.

"Intruders!"

She released Traq and sprang forward, pulling a rock out of her pocket that she'd grabbed outside the city. A man started climbing out, raising his gun up to aim at her.

She threw the rock at his face, still moving forward. He ducked and it missed, but gave her enough time to close the distance. She kicked him in the stomach, knocking him back into the door frame and then slammed his head against the corner of the door.

He tried to pull his gun up again, dazed, but she didn't give him the opportunity. She slammed him again, then let him fall limply to the ground. She noticed a vibro-blade strapped to his hip and grabbed it as he fell, drawing it loose.

She flicked her wrist, setting it into motion, and felt the comfortable thrum of the blade. It wasn't as long as her personal weapon, but it was nice having something she'd trained with her entire life.

Vivian continued forward, ducking behind the vehicle and out of sight of the other vehicle. Shots rang out from inside that second car, missing her by a wide margin, and she hoped missing Traq as well. With any luck, he was cowering low and out of sight and they wouldn't even notice him.

In either case, she needed to hurry. They knew she was here now and were doubtless calling in backup, and that made it all much more dangerous.

She stepped forward around the other side of the vehicle. The door was open and a passenger was stepping out. He was wearing a uniform and facing away from her. He had a pistol in his hand and started barking orders, trying to get his soldiers into position.

She stabbed in, hitting him in the lower back from behind. Her blade tore through his body, ripping it to shreds on the way through.

He tensed up and tried to turn, and she instantly recognized him. General Coley. He met her eyes, a look of confusion and fear on his face.

"You..." he muttered.

She didn't answer except to stare at him.

"What have you done?"

He slid forward, dead before he hit the ground. Vivian ducked down and grabbed the gun off of the ground next to him. She raised it up and fired into the car twice. The shots hit the driver, once in the shoulder and the other in his head. Then she aimed forward at the other vehicle farther away and fired at it as well, forcing the soldiers to duck back out of sight to avoid being hit.

"Come on!" Vivian shouted back at Traq.

She saw him climb up from the ground and start running toward her.

He moved around the back of the vehicle and she pointed for him to keep going. They were close to their destination and had to get inside the loading bay.

The other vehicles in the convoy had stopped and seemed to be coming back as well, probably to protect their general. She knew they had to hurry.

She waited until Traq was a good distance ahead of her and then ran to catch up. She fired off a couple of shots at the approaching vehicles and other soldiers, and then they were at the bay where her ship was being stored.

She sliced with the stolen vibro-blade and the lock crumbled to the floor. She kicked the door open and rushed inside. It was dark inside, but she didn't know where lights might be located.

She could see enough to find the way to her ship. The vehicles were parking outside, but they were too far away to get a clear sight on them.

She punched in the key code and the loading door slid open. She didn't have time to wait for the ramp, so she grabbed Traq and tossed him inside.

The vehicles were parked outside the open bay door now. She heard gunshots and shouts as the soldiers approached, but they weren't close enough to be accurate. Bullets thudded into the area around her, some hitting the ship's metal exterior.

She fired off a few suppressing shots of her own, spending the last of the ammunition, and then climbed up onto the ship behind Traq.

She slammed the button to close the ramp and ran to the cockpit and cycled the power. As soon as the ship powered on, it began pinging her with messages. They were all labeled and had been sent by Traq's uncle or Argus.

She ignored them for now, checking through the flight systems and making sure they were clear for takeoff. She was worried they might have installed a grounding system to keep them from flying, but it seemed that with the war, they hadn't had time. Doubtless they had never expected her to return.

As soon as she was certain the ship was flight ready, she took control of the ships guns and aimed for the roof. More contact requests were pinging in from the nearby flight towers, warning her that if she tried to leave, they would shoot her down, but she ignored those as well.

Two quick shots blasted a hole in the roof and she took off, heading straight up. They breached the building, then headed for the outer atmosphere.

She didn't know if anyone down on the planet was firing at her, but she doubted they would be able to manage a response like that given the battle already raging outside their city.

After a few seconds, they were out of range of any ground attacks. She allowed herself to relax and looked back down at the city below. It was lit up beneath her by the flood lights and searchlights, and those were punctuated by the occasional rocket blast and explosion.

The fence had been breached in multiple locations, and it looked chaotic. The battle looked like it would go on for a long while, but she was just glad to be clear of it. She had no idea which side would win, and she didn't particularly care either.

Of course, knowing that she had accidentally killed the main General for Delphi, she had to assume she wasn't helping their chances any.

Nothing she could do about that now. Her priority was keeping Traq safe and getting him as far away from Eldun as she could.

4

She scrolled through the messages once they were at a high enough altitude to start planning a warp lane jump. Worried messages from Jack and Argus. They knew about the war raging on Eldun and wanted to make sure she and Traq had made it off world all right.

She decided to call Argus later, once she'd had time to relax and get some rest. For now, though, she called Jack.

He answered immediately, ashen faced and worried. It looked like he hadn't slept in days.

"Vivian, are you all right? Is Traq all right?"

"We're fine," Vivian said. "You were right. I should have listened to you and steered clear of Eldun."

"What happened?"

"The war reached Delphi. Our ship was impounded, and we had to make a run for it. We got out, though, and everything is fine."

"How was Traq? Did he get in the way?"

Vivian glanced behind her. She didn't see Traq and assumed he had already gone to his quarters. No doubt he was sleeping and recovering.

"No," she said. "He was perfect. I'm not sure I would have made it off Eldun without him."

"Can I talk to him?"

"He's sleeping."

"Are you heading back to Jaril now?"

"Yes," Vivian said. "We'll be there in a few days."

"Okay," he said. "See you then."

She ended the connection and then plotted the course. Her little robot, TM, would actually handle the math for her. She clicked angrily at Vivian, berating her for taking so long and letting them impound the ship, but Vivian was too tired to deal with her just now.

Once they were safely in flight, she headed back to her chambers and rested. She had never been so exhausted in her entire life and felt like she could sleep for weeks. She also had never felt so conflicted.

She had undertaken this experiment to try and separate Traq from his uncle, but she realized now that had been a poor and selfish decision. What would happen to Traq if she was lost?

But she couldn't keep Jack around without filling him in about everything: the Ministry, the Order, everything. He would need to understand why she was pushing Traq so hard and what he represented.

Could she trust him with that? A misstep from Jack would likely get them both killed. But she didn't see any alternatives except for severing ties and never looking back.

A concern for another day. Right now, she had a much more pressing matter to attend to. Once she rested, she decided, she would call Argus. Maybe a couple of hours of sleep, though.

She was out as soon as her head hit the pillow.

Chapter 20
Sector 6 – Jaril
Vivian Drowel

1

"I don't think you know what you're asking."

"I know exactly what I'm asking for, Wade."

"It's suicide..."

"That's a bit melodramatic."

"No, it isn't. It's apt, given the circumstances. This is reckless."

"You think I don't know that?"

"They will kill you if they found out you even *suggested* it. Hell, they will kill *me* if they found out I didn't report you for just thinking about something like this. I can't do this."

"You're in charge of the Order's equipment and supplies. You can do anything."

"Not this," Wade said, then sighed. "This...this is..."

"I know," Vivian said, looking away from the communication device and letting out a sigh. She was on Jaril with Jack and Traq, having recovered for a few weeks from their ordeal on Eldun.

Her body was still sore, but she was more determined than ever to make this newfound goal a reality. The more she thought about everything that had happened, the surer she was she needed to see this through.

Originally, the goal had been to keep Traq out of the Ministry and protect him from ever receiving an implant. Now, however, she felt like they didn't have a choice but to make him more like the members of the *Ordo Mens Rea*.

Argus was back at the Ministry, hiding out in his chambers and speaking with her. He was on edge and nervous, more so than normal because of the seriousness of her request.

"To give an implant to a non-sanctioned child would be blaspheming against the Ministry. I know the creeds, Wade. I know all of the Ministry laws. But he has potential."

"Too much potential," Wade replied, rubbing his face with his hands. "I saw him that day, Vivian. In the woods. He did things without an implant that only a few of us can do with one."

"You didn't see this," she said. "On Eldun, he exhibited more power, and he did other things, too. Not just telekinesis. I think he is telepathic too."

"Impossible."

"So we thought," Vivian replied. "But he is something else entirely. We need to do this."

"The records are strictly monitored."

"You can change them."

"There are backups."

"You can change those, too."

"The backups have backups!"

Vivian said. "I get it, Wade. It's dangerous. But we need to do this. We need to find out what his limits are and what he is capable of."

Argus was silent for a long moment.

"Do you know how the implants work?"

"They enhance our abilities. For me, telekinesis. They make it possible for me to use my power."

"Yes, but do you know *how* it works?"

"No. I don't know," Vivian replied. "If anyone told me, I've forgotten."

Argus shook his head. "You haven't forgotten. No one told you. The thing is…I don't know either."

"What do you mean?"

"I don't know how they work," he reiterated.

"You maintain them," she said. "They don't trust you to know?"

"No. They don't know either."

She hesitated. "What?"

"No one understands exactly how they work. At first I thought it was a closely guarded secret and they just weren't telling me, but I found out that no one actually knows. I mean, we know how to replicate and grow them, but—"

"Grow?" Vivian asked incredulously.

Wade pursed his lips. "It isn't important. What is important is that we *think* about what to do next and make a clear and rational decision."

"What are you saying? What do you think we should do?"

"Maybe we should bring him in. If you think he is as powerful as you say...this might be beyond us."

"No," she said. "That isn't happening. You said yourself: The Order isn't accepting any new students. Not now. Maybe never again. The Minister blames us personally for Darius's fall, and they would lobotomize Traq the second he showed up."

"Maybe that is for the best."

"Are you even listening to yourself? He doesn't need to join the *Ordo Mens Rea*. Just give him the implant."

"You're missing the point."

"Clearly."

"Do you know why we are called the *Ordo Mens Rea*?"

"No," Vivian replied. "But again, it doesn't seem—"

"It means the Order of the Guilty Mind."

"Right..."

"But before we were the *Ordo Mens Rea* and the Ministry adopted us, we were a heretical cult."

"What?" Vivian asked, surprised. "I've never heard that."

"Of course you haven't. This isn't canon and the Ministry scrubbed it from memory. It was over eight hundred years ago. They found our cult on a distant planet using the implants and worshipping...well, worshipping something. The records aren't clear on that. We fought them. They won. And they adapted us and brought us into the Ministry.

"Then they purged our history, removing all records of what we were prior to the Ministry. But Vivian, it was bad. The things we could do...the people we hurt. You cannot repeat this Vivian. Any of it. It's heretical information, and even whispering things like this could get everyone killed. Everything I'm telling you is dangerous."

"Then why are you telling me?"

"Because I want you to understand just what you are asking. There are many within the Ministry—and I mean *many*—who think executing all of us and ending what the Ministry began so long ago would be a good idea. All of us. We don't fit into their sacrosanct view of the galaxy."

"And you think the Minister is one of them?"

"I don't think. I know he is. But right now we are in the First Citizen's good graces. We represent the Shields and his ambivalence keeps us alive. Our usefulness outweighs the Minister's hatred of us. But, what you're suggesting where Traq is concerned…it could tip the scales. If they find out I sent one of the implants out of the Ministry…"

"And he would kill us?" Vivian asked. "You really think he would murder all thirty thousand of us?

Wade hesitated. "I wouldn't put it past him."

Vivian shook her head. "It's worth the risk, Wade. I'm telling you, Traq is something else. He changes everything we think we know. I will keep Traq away from the Ministry, and you will change the records. No one need ever know he has an implant. But we cannot pass up this opportunity."

"Gods, you are persistent," Wade said, scratching his chin. He was silent for a minute, staring at the wall and thinking. "Fine. I'll do it. I'll modify the registry and get Traq his implant. Where do you want me to send it?

"Where would work?"

He thought about it for a minute. "There is a doctor on Terminus who used to work at the Ministry. He put the implants in, and he left the Ministry on not so great terms. There are spies watching him, but most were recalled when the Union split off from the Republic."

"You think he will help?"

"I doubt you intend to give him a choice," Wade said. "When I ship the item, it'll arrive after only a few days. You need to be there and make sure he doesn't report it."

"I can do that."

"He might need some convincing that it is in his best interest…but, whatever happens, he *cannot* report this to the Ministry or we are all doomed."

"Okay."

"I'll send you an address. But Vivian, once this is done, there is no going back."

“I know.”

“I’m not sure you do,” Argus Wade said, shaking his head. “I don’t think you understand what is at stake…But Vivian, if this goes wrong, you will.”

Epilogue
Oliver

"Are those the new shipping manifests?" Oliver asked.

"Yeah."

"What did we get?"

"New uniforms," Jim replied. The two men were walking into a shipping class freighter named *Spotrunner*. It was one of six courier ships that traveled with Jim's Flagship, *Infinity*. Jim had picked up a data pad from the nearest stack of boxes and was going through the inventory of what *Spotrunner* would carry to the flagship. Jim liked to go over the manifests personally, despite hiring thirty-six people assigned to only that responsibility.

It wasn't that Jim didn't trust his crew. He was just terrified that something would go wrong. *Thorough to the point of paranoia*, Jim thought. But, then again, he didn't really mind doing this task himself. Things were going well, and for him, getting a chance to see the shipments personally was like being on holiday: *It's all ours.*

Five years ago Jim was nobody. Then Oliver walked into his life—*stumbled* was probably a better description—and now Jim controlled the strongest fleet in the Indeil Kingdom. Over two hundred ships.

But it wasn't all fun and games. It had come as something of a shock to find out how ill prepared he was for such a position. He had military experience, but nothing compared to the sheer scale of a war fleet. Luckily, the fleet he inherited was already fairly well maintained. Jim kept the same crews intact and had slowly begun filling out the ranks.

"You're joking, right?" Oliver asked, glancing over his shoulder to read the pad.

"Not at all," Jim said. "Just uniforms."

Oliver cleared his throat. "Where are the guns I ordered?"

"I cancelled that order," Jim said, raising an eyebrow at his friend. "We don't need more guns."

"But those were *new* guns," Oliver retorted. "You can't expect me to use a gun more than once, can you? They are disposable, right?"

Jim didn't reply, but he did smile slightly. "I don't expect you to use them at all. The last time you went to the firing range, you couldn't even hit the target."

"It kept moving," Oliver protested.

"It's locked in place," Jim said. "It can't move."

"Well, then it should have moved," Oliver said.

"In any case, we don't need more guns. The armory is full. Yet our soldiers *do* need something to wear."

Our personal hangar, Jim reminded himself. *Hell, it's our goddamned spaceport.* Oliver had purchase the Jaril municipal spaceport just over a year earlier. He'd convinced Jim to use their fleet primarily for shipping goods around the Kingdom, so most of their investment was in owning the ports that connected their trade routes.

Oliver pried off the top of a nearby crate.

"No knives?"

"Nope?"

"Grenades? Frying pans? How are we supposed to kill people, Jim?"

Jim sighed. "The Kingdom hasn't been at war for eighty years."

Jim's data pad beeped. He checked the feed: Another transport ship had landed safely on Immis. It was dropping off their cargo now.

Life had been good the last few years. The marriage to Lady Margaret was a huge event. He expanded his popularity with the civilians and solidified his position in the Admiralty. And no one—at least publicly—dared speak out against the lady for her choice of consort. They received a steady stream of recruits and were currently in the negotiations to acquire their seventh Capital Warship.

He had surpassed Brutus Volt within the first year. Two months ago, Oliver had purchased the ship that put them past Hektor Menschen. With the way things were going, it wouldn't be long before he outnumbered them both combined. *And how that must anger Hektor.*

The thought brought a smile to his lips.

How angry will he be after today? Jim wondered. But he wondered even more how Oliver would feel about it. I hope he isn't offended. His feelings are fairly obvious to everyone but him. Am I stepping over the bounds in our friendship?

He wouldn't know until after he'd gone through with it.

A few minutes passed as Jim verified the manifest against what was in the crate. This box was loaded with expensive uniforms. Bridge officers. At least Jim didn't have a lot of positions left to fill on the ships they already had.

"How's Becka?" Oliver asked, pulling Jim from his thoughts. Jim glanced at the data pad in his hand and dropped it back on the stack of boxes in front of him.

"She's great. Fantastic, really," Jim said, stretching out his back and yawning. "A little ball of energy. She never stops moving."

"And you barely move at all anymore. A fair trade."

My damn foot, Jim cursed. Physical therapy wasn't working very well, and it would be a short time before he needed a cane. *God help me if I'm ever resigned to a walker...*

"And Emily is gorgeous," Jim continued, deciding to ignore Oliver's statement. Emily was a newborn, barely a month old. A little pink ball of joy that terrified Jim. Becka had just turned two. "Absolutely gorgeous. I never imagined being away from them would be this hard."

"It's only for a few weeks at a time," Oliver said.

Jim said. "Yeah, I know," he gestured to the boxes. "There should be three hundred and twenty-one uniforms."

"Three hundred and twenty-one? That's a strange number."

"It's how many we needed," Jim said. He began limping along the row of boxes. The cargo bay was twenty meters long and sixteen wide. Right now it was empty except for these crates. He slid the top off another crate and leafed through the uniforms, nodding to himself.

"These are high quality," Oliver said, picking one up and shaking it loose. "You spared no expense."

"We have the funds."

"I'm glad you asked first."

"It's my fleet," Jim said, not looking at Oliver.

"But *our* money," Oliver said. "And I earn most of it."

Jim shrugged. "Fair enough. I'll ask next time."

Oliver shook his head. "I'm joking. I don't really care. Just don't spend us into poverty," he said and then grinned. "And next time don't veto my gun order."

Jim nodded absently. He continued down the line, checking the next crate of uniforms.

"Kids are tough," he said absently.

"Yeah."

"I just wish Margaret..."

Jim trailed off midsentence, tensing up. He glanced around, making sure they were alone. He hated speaking about his reclusive wife, especially if he might be overheard. Oliver knew everything, of course, but they rarely spoke about it in public. "It's not that..." he started again quieter. "She just..."

"I know," Oliver said, patting him on the shoulder. "But she won't stay that way. She's just having trouble adjusting."

The somber tone held for a long minute. Oliver glanced past him at one of the larger crates. "What's in that one?"

"It's the odd uniform," Jim said. "A new bridge officer for *Infinity*."

"I thought we didn't have any open positions on the flagship," Oliver said.

"We don't," Jim said, "but when this offer came my way, I decided to make an exception."

"A position on the flagship? That's quite the exception," Oliver said. "Who is it?"

"She should be here any minute."

"You didn't consult me?"

"No," Jim said, waving his hand at one of the guards near the cargo bay door. "I forgot."

"Oh hell, it's not—"

Oliver stopped speaking, eyes fixated on the cargo door. A brunette in an expensive dress suit had just walked through. Her hair was pulled back from her face into a bun and she was wearing high heels. Jim had only seen her a few times, but he knew her brother too well to not recognize her: Elizabeth Menschen. When she spoke to him about a possible position, he'd fallen all over himself to bring her on board.

It was only after that he'd realized his mistake. She and Oliver had some sort of relationship years earlier. Rumor was they'd had a falling-out.

"She offered to sign on. I told her I'd think about it. But there's nothing to think about. She's Hektor's sister. I couldn't possibly turn her away."

Oliver blinked. "Does Hektor know?"

"I'm sure he'll find out. And to be honest, I don't really care. She's a grown woman."

"And you never even thought to mention it to me," Oliver said.

Jim sighed. "Look, if I'd known about your...relationship...I would have said something. But the truth is, this wasn't something I could pass up. That we could pass up. Just having her here will keep her brother off my back."

"I'm pretty sure she hates me," Oliver said.

"Why?" Jim asked.

"Because she said she did. The last time we spoke."

"Well, she never mentioned it. And she has to know that you're my First Officer."

Suddenly, Oliver burst out laughing. "Wait...this is her uniform, right?"

"Yes. That's why I asked her to come today."

"I'll be back," Oliver said, hurrying toward the far door leading into the cockpit. There was a side exit up there, leading to the street. "And whatever you do, don't tell her the uniform came."

"What?" Jim asked, completely caught off guard. He was expecting some kind of response, but this wasn't it.

"Five minutes," Oliver replied. "Just keep her busy for five minutes."

Jim watched him disappear and shook his head. Heels clipped behind him and he turned, bowing to Elizabeth Menschen.

"Where's he off to?" she asked, narrowing her eyes. Jim could only shrug in response. "Did he not know I was...?" she asked, her voice trailing off. There was an edge of hurt in her eyes. "Was he upset?"

"I think he had to go pick something up. He'll be back shortly."

"Ah," she said. "Well, you asked me to come today."

"Yes," Jim said. *To give you your uniform,* he didn't say. He struggled to think of something else to say, but he'd never been good at small talk.

Damn it, Oliver. How the hell am I supposed to keep her busy?

A minute dragged past.

Jim cleared his throat.

"So..." Elizabeth said. "Did you have anything in particular...?"

"Yes," Jim said. "I mean no. We're just waiting for some more recruits to arrive so we can travel to *Infinity.* So yes, I suppose there was something we needed to do before leaving. Are you ready to leave today, or do you need more time to prepare?"

"I have everything I need outside. I can leave whenever," she said, then hesitated. "Is Oliver...?"

"He's okay with this," Jim said. "I think."

"That's good," she said with a nod. "After..." She trailed off.

They each scanned the room. Another minute passed awkwardly. Elizabeth cleared her throat. "I...um...am not involved in my brother's dealings...so if you were thinking I would...spy..."

"Oh no, nothing like that," Jim said, deflated. That was exactly what he *was* hoping for.

"Good," Elizabeth said, glancing around again. She was clearly waiting for him to continue, but he couldn't think of anything else to add. "That's good...needless to say, my brother wasn't happy when I told him. He's basically written me out of the family."

"We'll help you recover anything you lost in joining us," Jim said. "I was never intending for your contributions to involve your family in any way."

"You have my thanks," Elizabeth said.

Time moved slowly.

"So then why?" she asked.

"Why what?"

"Why bring me on? You *must* be worried that I will betray you to Hektor. And Oliver...I'm not sure he's forgiven me. I couldn't believe you said yes."

Jim hesitated. *This isn't going well.* "To be perfectly honest, I haven't given it much thought. Oliver is the one who worries about those sorts of things."

"He did agree to this arrangement, though? I don't want to step on anyone's toes..."

"He, um...I'm sure he will agree."

Or, at least, I hope he will.

Where the hell are you, Oliver?

Jim cleared his throat.

"So...are you looking forward to—?"

"I'm back," Oliver called, waving at them as he stepped through the hangar door. He didn't look angry, for which Jim was duly grateful.

Thank God, Jim thought.

"Thank God," Elizabeth mumbled.

Oliver came up to them, puffing and putting his hands on his knees.

"Where did you go?" Elizabeth asked, a note of impatience in her voice as she crossed her arms.

"Oh, I had to check our takeoff status," Oliver lied. "We run a pretty tight ship here."

"Is that so?" Elizabeth asked. She seemed uncomfortable. She was as worried about this meeting as I was, Jim realized. Worried what Oliver might say.

"We'll be gone a few weeks. Jim's daughter is only a month old," Oliver explained. "We never go too far away if we don't have to."

"Oh, I'd forgotten about the baby. Congratulations. I'll be sure to send Margaret my regards and a gift. Does she have enough clothes?"

"Three closets full," Jim said.

Elizabeth smiled. "Only three?" She glanced around. "I'll send a few more." She hesitated, looking at Oliver and then the ground. "I don't want to impose. Jim said you were not aware of this arrangement, and if it makes you uncomfortable..."

Oliver waved his hands dismissively in the air. "No, no. Any offer Jim has made to you, I second completely. I've missed you, Elizabeth. And I know that when you set me up to have me killed, there were no hard feelings."

"I tried as hard as I could to warn you," Elizabeth said, wringing her hands. "And I knew that if *I* didn't set you up, my brother would find some other way. And I was worried..."

"Wait," Jim said. "What?"

They ignored him.

"I said a lot of horrible things," Elizabeth said, looking down. "And I've regretted it ever since."

"But you had to be convincing," Oliver replied. He stepped forward and gently took her hands, lifting her chin to look her in the eyes. "And you slipped me the key before they tossed me in the river."

"What river?" Jim asked. "You never told me any of this."

Oliver waved his hand in dismissal. "It wasn't important. All is forgiven, Elizabeth. Welcome aboard *Infinity*."

Phew, Jim thought. This could have gone so much—

"There *is* just one problem," Oliver said.

"What?" Elizabeth asked, narrowing her eyes.

"We don't allow anyone on the bridge who isn't in proper attire."

"Oh?"

"And unfortunately, there was a mix-up with the recent shipment. Your uniform hasn't arrived yet. But don't worry. I have acquired a suitable replacement for you to wear in the interim."

Oliver fished in his pocket for a second, grinning.

"Where is it?" Elizabeth asked.

Oliver drew out a pair of diamond earrings and a matching necklace. They were expensive, gleaming in the drop ships lights.

Those have to cost a hundred thousand credits...Jim realized.

Oliver handed them to Elizabeth.

"Here it is," he said. "It's somewhat revealing, I know. But not at *all* constricting."

Elizabeth's eyes went wide, and she burst out laughing.

"I've missed you, Oly," she said, accepting the gift.

Even Jim couldn't help but smile.

Jayson

"What happens now?" he asked, sitting in his quarters on Alderson. His body was still sore and beat up after the events that had taken place, but he was starting to recover.

They had been back from the research facility for about a week, and already travel preparations were being drawn up for their excursion to Regamon. They would go in separate groups and unite on the planet.

It would be a dangerous mission, considering how well protected Regamon was in Sector Two. They were going to be briefed over the next few months about exactly what to expect from the planet, and

Bret was being briefed in explicit weaknesses in their security network and how to hack their grids.

It would be a long mission, with the intention being to ramp up their efforts over the course of a year. By the time they left, he knew, the goal was that the economy of Regamon and Sector Two would be crippled.

Ambitious, he knew, and incredibly dangerous.

He was excited and apprehensive at the same time. Sector Two was notorious for being one of the richest planets in the galaxy, nearly rivaling Axis in wealth and privilege. They would never expect for it to be targeted by terrorists, which was what made their plan possible: their own arrogance would be their downfall.

"Now you will begin tearing the Republic down," Alexander said. "Captain Grove will be patrolling near Regamon while you are there, and your job will be to turn the planet against her."

"Subterfuge?"

Alexander nodded. "It isn't going to be easy. I'm putting you in charge of the mission, which means you have complete autonomous control once you are on the planet. There will be no contact from or with us until after you have completed this mission."

"What, exactly, is the mission?"

Alexander smiled at him, shaking his head. "You'll see."

Captain Grove

"You knew it would go like that," Captain Kristi Grove accused, pointing a finger at Jamir. They were in her quarters, one of the few places she could speak openly with her manservant.

She was furious with Abdullah for pardoning the criminal. She was even more furious, however, for the smug way in which Jamir had planned it all out. He had orchestrated and manipulated everything, she was certain. Even herself.

And she did *not* like to be manipulated.

She had been certain that Abdullah would execute the rapist Gregory Tillman, or else she never would have given him control over the situation. Jamir had assured her that Abdullah would make the right decision, but in the end, her First Officer had pardoned the man.

"I did?"

"That's why you wanted Abdullah to make the decision. You knew he would let the man live. You *knew*."

"Seven years is a long sentence," Jamir replied. "Ensign Tillman will miss out on much of his life because of his crime and be expelled from the ship immediately when his sentence is over."

"It isn't enough. I should have him executed anyway."

"Then you would be undermining your own First Officer."

"If I'd known Abdullah wouldn't have the backbone—"

"No," Jamir interrupted.

She raised an eyebrow at him, shocked he would dare interrupt her.

"No?"

"The crew aboard this ship is terrified of you."

"They should be. I want their respect, but I'll tolerate their fear."

Jamir ignored her. "Yet they love Abdullah as much as they hate you."

"And you think that's a good thing?"

"It is a necessary thing. They will be loyal to him, and he will be loyal to you. You aren't looking for a puppet in your First Officer. You are looking for a leader who can inspire people. The soldiers will think of him as a leader who has their best interests at heart. Having him in the position that he is in will give you free rein to do the things you want to do while maintaining crew morale and loyalty. This is the best way to accomplish your agendas on behalf of the Republic."

"You're saying that Abdullah is a tool for me to use."

"In a sense," Jamir admitted. "You need someone like him as much as the Republic needs someone like you."

"So I should let him make more decisions like this? Pardon the crew for their crimes," she asked.

"On the contrary, you should *encourage* him to make decisions like this. He has a good heart and a strong will. I feared for a while that his fear of you would override his moral compass, but I can see the strength in him. He will bring out the best in the people under his command. You need to trust that this is in your best interest.

Captain Grove frowned, thinking. She hated the idea of letting criminals walk free, but she also knew better than to ignore the advice Jamir was giving her. This was exactly why her family had purchased him and why she kept him around.

"Very well. We will do things your way," she said. "For now."

Abdullah Al Hakir

Living on *Denigen's Fist* had turned into a constantly terrifying experience for Abdullah. He felt like he was walking on egg shells, and he was terrified of what would happen when the Captain finally turned her attention to him.

He knew she would bring the hammer down, eventually, but for now she wouldn't even speak to him. He spent his time with Eddie—who was pleased with the decision he'd made—and his soldiers, but he didn't dare go to the bridge.

Nor did Captain Grove ask for him. He wondered if she was planning out who would replace him.

He tried to occupy himself by keeping busy. In a few weeks, they would leave Axis and head to Regamon, and he would get some time away from the ship. It would be a relaxing vacation and relationship-building exercise. No doubt the Captain would be too busy rubbing elbows with the important people of the galaxy to worry about him.

He hoped...

In any case, he was at least proud of himself that he'd come to the right decision. He could live with himself for what he had done.

How long that would be, however, he didn't know.

Vivian

Vivian flew their little ship, *Junker*, down toward the surface of Terminus, a planet she hadn't spent much time on before. It was one she didn't have a lot of respect for in the grand scheme of things: a lawless and brutal planet notorious for rampant crime, rivaled only by Daer. It was a smuggler's haven and den of iniquity.

But it was also the only place she would be able to go to get Traq what he needed. She hated the idea of being back in the Republic, but she would do anything to find out exactly what Traq was capable of.

Technically, Terminus was under the control of the Union, though it certainly didn't consider itself to be the puppet of any government. She doubted they answered any better to Darius than they had to the First Citizen. It was a dangerous place, and she would need to be careful if she was going to bring Traq out the other side.

"This is Terminus?" Traq asked, sitting in the copilot's chair.

He had recovered from the ordeal on Eldun and was in much higher spirits, basically returning to his old self. His uncle, Jack, was resting in the back of the plane, having flown them most of the way here. Vivian still hadn't decided if she was going to trust him, but she did know that she needed him. For now, at least.

Traq hadn't managed to manifest any powers since leaving Eldun behind, and he barely seemed to remember most of what had happened. When she asked him about it, his memory of how he had done things was vague and disoriented, solidifying her belief that he needed the implant.

"This is Terminus," she agreed. "A wretched place."

"What are we doing here?"

She hesitated, not sure what to tell him. "We're going to get you something," she said. "You'll have a surgery and then you'll be able to do things."

"What kind of things?"

"I don't know yet," she said. "More things like on Eldun, but we'll find out after. That's why we are here. Are you ready?"

He shrugged. "I guess so."

Everything would change after this, she knew. Traq would change, and she prayed he would still be the lovable kid she knew.

But she also understood that the implant could have an adverse effect on the personality of people it was put into. There was a chance that the Traq that woke up would be entirely different from the one she brought to Terminus. If that happened...

She didn't know what she would do.

She hoped it wouldn't happen.

End of Book II
Lincoln Cole

About the Author

Lincoln Cole is a Columbus-based author who enjoys traveling and has visited many different parts of the world, including Australia and Cambodia, but always returns home to his pugamonster puppy, Luther, and family. His love for writing was kindled at an early age through the works of Isaac Asimov and Stephen King and he enjoys telling stories to anyone who will listen.